NIGHT FLIGHTS

Also by Matt Cohen

THE COLOURS OF WAR
WOODEN HUNTERS
THE DISINHERITED
JOHNNY CRACKLE SINGS

NIGHT FLIGHTS

Stories New and Selected

MATT COHEN

Doubleday Canada Limited, Toronto, Ontario
DOUBLEDAY & COMPANY, INC., GARDEN CITY, NEW YORK
1978

"Columbus and the Fat Lady," "Janice," "Country Music," and, in a different form, "The Toy Pilgrim," first appeared in COLUMBUS AND THE FAT LADY, Anansi Press, copyright © 1972 by Matt Cohen.

"Glass Eyes and Chickens" first appeared in *Harrowsmith,* copyright © 1976 by Matt Cohen. "The Hanged Man" first appeared in *Harrowsmith,* copyright © 1977 by Matt Cohen.

"The Secret" first appeared in *New Canadian Stories 1974,* Oberon Press, copyright © 1974 by Matt Cohen.

"Heyfitz" first appeared in the *Canadian Forum,* copyright © 1977 by Matt Cohen.

"A Literary History of Anton" first appeared in *The Story So Far,* Coach House Press, copyright © 1976 by Matt Cohen.

"Death of a Friend" first appeared in *Saturday Night,* copyright © 1976 by Matt Cohen.

Library of Congress Cataloging in Publication Data

Cohen, Matthew, 1942–
    Night flights.

       CONTENTS: The cure.—Brothers.—Columbus and the fat lady. [etc.]
       I. Title.
PZ4.C67725Ni 1978 [PR9199.3C58] 813'.5'4
ISBN: 0-385-13333-2
ISBN: 0-385-13334-0 paperback
Library of Congress Catalog Card Number 77–89879

CONTENTS

NIGHT FLIGHTS

THE CURE

Eliot Simon's memories of his father were intensely formal: conversations across cold distances of furniture and carpets; meetings arranged to fit around more important engagements; silences for which there were first excuses, then apologies, but finally no explanation at all other than the mutual and natural hostility that seemed to underlie all their relations.

Eliot was therefore annoyed but not surprised when his lawyer wrote to say that his father had begun a court action to stop payment of his trust monies. This action, according to his lawyer, would not be dropped until Eliot commenced divorce proceedings against his wife; *the felonious and criminally indicted Lara Simon* was how they referred to her. Through the whole day, Eliot thought about this situation, let it rotate in his mind during his exercises, while he painted, even in the midst of a long sunny walk along the ocean front. And then, in the late afternoon, sitting quietly in his doctor's office, watching his hands while he spoke, Eliot told about the letter, about his plans to go East to divorce his wife.

"I'm not sure you should leave at this time," the doctor said.

"I have to."

"Well," said the doctor. "I'll be here to welcome you back."

* * *

He flew from San Francisco to New York on the 9:00 A.M. flight. He sat in the first-class section and spent most of the flight observing his hands, which were long, slim-fingered, and nervously twisted into each other. His name was Eliot Simon. He was twenty-seven years old, wearing a white linen suit that set off his pink-patterned Cardin tie; and his hair, sandy and thin, was brushed back to emphasize a pale, almost effete face, a face that was in this year, 1976, fifty years out of date, a face that could have belonged to a transoceanic 1920s dandy, with its narrow, straight features, freckles over the bridge of the nose that would eventually be patrician, candy-blue eyes that reflected, as did everything else about him, money.

He was looking at his hands, and he thought he had spent a lot of time in the past two years doing only that, aiming his eyes toward these particular patches of his being, so much time that he hardly saw them now. And although he could inspect the territory that was familiar, observe the straight, narrow bones that connected his knuckles to his wrists, bones that as he grew older were gradually being lapped by veins, if he closed his eyes and tried to remember his own hands, asked himself questions about where the skin might be particularly red, where the pores were beginning to enlarge, he wouldn't know the answers.

Nervous. He was watching his hands and he knew it was a sign of his own nervousness. On most days at this time he was in the gymnasium, testing his muscles against the steel-springed exercisers that were bolted to the wall, riding the stationary bicycle, even lifting the weights he had so carefully avoided the first few months. And thinking of this, remembered the last time he had seen himself in the mirror, skinny still but beginning to be almost muscular, his arms and legs roped with new strength, the muscles surrounding those larger bones the way his veins surrounded these small ones.

Sitting sometimes beside him was the only other occupant of the first-class section, the stewardess. Her face was round and covered with shining makeup. Though her eyes, too, were blue, they were a much darker color, a deep sea-water blue that was emphasized by the mascara and long black lashes that surrounded.

"It's a nice day," Eliot said. His teeth were very slightly

crooked, in a way that others had found charming. "You like flying on a good day like this."

"Night flights are better," the stewardess said. "They're more romantic."

"I flew at night once. I flew from Chicago to New Zealand." His voice, like the rest of him, was light and clear: a shallow voice he had to be careful with, or it could sound brittle.

"New Zealand," repeated the stewardess professionally. "I've always heard that was a nice place."

* * *

The entire situation was taking place in his mind. He was aware of that. It was reminding him of something the doctor had said, a long windy speech about the processes of thinking, about the subtle workings of the human mind, about adult responsibility and mental health.

The particular window he was looking out, the window of his hotel room, which was on the sixteenth floor and was, according to the instructions he had given his lawyer, at the farthest possible remove from the elevator, had been blotted and stained by successive layers of pollution and rain, giving the city, even the blue sky now hazed over, a vaguely smeared look, as if his eyes couldn't properly focus.

"Eliot Simon," he said. The sharp sound of his own voice woke him up, reminded him that the situation was also taking place in this hotel room, completely out of his control.

Lara Simon, for she insisted on continuing to use his name even though she had, at least technically speaking, deserted him two years before, was the precise focus of this chaos.

"You're looking very nice, Eliot."

"Thank you." He turned away from the window and wondered what she thought of the fact that he talked to himself sometimes, even in public.

"I like you in that white suit. You look nice in white."

"Thank you," he said again.

"You really do dress very well for a man. I think there's something sinister about that, don't you? I mean, it's not as if you were queer."

"No." His voice broke and he coughed, trying to make it sound natural. The doctor had told him that being nervous in front of his wife was only a matter of symptoms. It had reminded him of something he had read somewhere, that the only cure for male-pattern baldness was castration. The symptoms were embarrassingly ordinary: shaking hands, inappropriate sweating. The idea was to control each one individually; the doctor had said that if you learned to control things they didn't exist any more. Very dangerous, Eliot had thought, intrapsychic fascism.

"What are you thinking about? You know, you never tell me what you're thinking." She was sounding annoyed, an old trick she had to make him concentrate on her. He was reminded that her face, pale and angular, was enough like his in a smoother and more modern way for them to be sometimes mistaken for brother and sister, as if their marriage that had been incestuous in spirit had been so also in fact. He looked at her face and finally, for the first time since she had come to his room, their eyes met. Hers were brown, deep and sympathetic. He knew that if he kept watching her, he would slowly drift into them. This even while he was remembering one of her more offensive lovers, a white-sandaled car dealer who wore an astrological pendant that had, at the beach, literally banged against his collarbone as he walked.

Eliot turned away, focused on his hands, and for once kept them still. And watched them, not shaking, carefully extract a cigarette from his gold case, light it with a matching lighter, and then, still in complete and absolute steady control, place it carefully between his lips as if it were the only thing to be considered.

"Have you seen your father yet?"

"Tomorrow." When he thought about his father, he reminded himself of attitudes even more antique than his clothes and the set of his face. He reminded himself, as he had once explained to the doctor, of the extinction of dinosaurs who had grown so large because, in a desperate attempt to eliminate sibling and other rivalries, and to achieve their own particular mental health, they were forced to engross themselves by eating the other members of their family.

* * *

He was on a holding pattern. That was another of the doctor's gifts. "Imagine you are a television set. Your face is composed of millions of dots, ready to be activated by your emotions."

During this, and their other conversations, Eliot had been seated in a brown quilted leather chair that was to the side of the window, enough displaced so he could feel securely blanketed by the shadows of late afternoon.

"Your mind is the scanner, broadcasting feelings onto your face. If you can just learn to control that, to keep your face in repose—"

The telephone rang. The sound at first startled him, then he adjusted to it. Soon the noise stopped and the orange light commenced to flash, to tell him there was a message at the switchboard.

He went into the bathroom and closed the door. He sat on the side of the bathtub, first carefully protecting the seat of his white trousers with a towel. In retrospect, the doctor who had seemed so essential was now becoming a bald, gleaming globe.

He avoided the mirror, took a deep breath, and looked down at the tile floor. "Well," he said aloud. "What do you know?" Vowels were the hard part; the open vowels strained the walls of his thin voice, tried to break it apart. "Walls," he practiced. "Old walls wallow in the willows."

In the hospital his craziness had been of the boring variety. At the worst moments, even during the transitions from one drug to the next, he never saw visions, heard footsteps, dreamed of monsters that didn't exist.

Others painted therapeutically. Formless colors poured onto the paper; as if the construction-grade sheets were garbage cans for their psyches; as if the energy of the universe had somehow gotten into them, shattered them, was trampling them out of humanness, out of anything defined.

He himself only painted things, inexpert renditions of objects that could be recognized, such as wooden chairs. Even when he had been most involved with drugs, which was not in the hospital but in a beach house with Lara, where they looked out at the Pacific Ocean while imbibing his mother's estate in the form of morphine and cocaine, he had never seen real visions, only ordinary things lit up from the inside, as if each object, each plant, even each human being, had its own private sun.

The telephone rang again, and this time, unaware of himself, he walked out of the bathroom and picked up the receiver.

"Eliot, where have you been?"

"Right here."

He stood with his eyes squinting out the window. Between the tall and narrow rows of buildings, the sun was setting in an explosive scarlet haze. They had caught him in an elevator, coming down from the top floor of the St. Francis Hotel in San Francisco. Looking out the glassed elevator shaft to the city, then walking into the arms of the two detectives. His hair longer then, his white linen suits handmade by Lara. He closed his eyes and let the long horizontal rays from the sun play upon his lids, burn through, make smooth and buzzing circles in the bones of his skull.

* * *

His lawyer's name was Sammy Sparrow, a name that suited him because although he tried to look eccentric on the outside, he was, Simon knew, perfectly neat within, rows of precedents and figures carefully filed in available places, always ready to be cited.

Now Sparrow, dressed in tattered blue jeans and an old painting shirt, was lecturing him on the conservative virtues.

"You've got to think of your family," he said to Eliot. "I mean for Christ's sake you're *Eliot Simon*. You can't let that crazy bitch take from you."

"Who's crazy?" Sammy had come and rescued him from the police station, joked about the bruises under his eyes. But that was two years ago, and now Eliot wished that Sammy would dress like other lawyers. "I don't even know how they let you into the hotel, looking like that," he said distractedly.

"She's a vampire," Sammy said. "You know what a vampire is?"

"No."

"Someone who sucks blood."

This brought to Eliot's mind two images: the first was a sudden vision of Lara at his throat, not sucking blood but clinging, both of them wrapped in her cool percale sheets and pouring the afternoon into each other; and the second, which was maybe closer to what Sammy meant, was a picture of not a tooth but a needle, a long needle pulling away from his thigh, blood coming off in tiny dainty tears, an elegant line of crimson tears dotting its way down the white flesh of his thigh to his knee. He coughed and tried to find his voice. The doctor had told him that he could learn to control the flow of his own mind, that there was no reason he should subject himself to every flash of longing or pain that found its way into his attention.

Sparrow was laughing, a conspiratorial giggle that made Eliot want to move even farther away, which was impossible because he was already pressed, so angry he could hardly catch his breath, against the painted wooden sill of the hotel window.

* * *

It was the evening of his first day in New York and he was eating dinner with his lawyer. The situation was new now, and it was at this moment very simple, very simply the situation of his choosing between the trout, which he suspected of being imported from Canada, frozen and contaminated with mercury, and the filet, which had probably gained its robust flavor with the aid of steroids and hormones.

"I'll just have a salad," he said to the waiter.

"Eat," Sammy insisted. "You'll die if you don't eat."

"In North America more people die from obesity than malnutrition."

"Not you."

"I'll also have the consommé," Eliot said in appeasement. "Do you think hormones dissolve?" There was a silence. "I'm sorry," Eliot said. "I must have been thinking something else." Lara would have known what to do about Sammy, how to manipulate him into a more suitable posture, obeisance to the family whose fortune had, in an absent-minded moment, provided him with a lifetime of his raggedy blue jeans and painted shirts.

The waiter came back with the soup. It swayed in its wide-brimmed bowl, abruptly reminding Eliot of the sea, of the fact that, in California, each night at this time he walked down to the shore and spent the evening watching the sky change colors. At the beach where he went, a sparsely-peopled place that was near the sanitarium but not of it, the driftwood logs dotted the sand in hyphenated rows, like benches, and as the colors deepened from red to the deep Pacific blue, he would feel a vague sense of brotherhood with the others who watched. Sometimes bottles of cheap red wine were passed around, or better, the smell of marijuana would cut deep through the still summer air, sharp and nostalgic, and he would sit and smoke with strangers, comforted by their loosening chatter.

"You're not listening."

"I'm here." Soup had given way to a cornucopia of greens. He found himself balancing a fork skeptically between his fingers, poking it among the endive and crushed parsley. "You were saying that you were worried about my divorce."

"About your *hypothetical* divorce," Sammy said. "About the fact that you hate to confront Lara with anything."

"She's already agreed."

"What?"

"She agreed to everything this afternoon. In the hotel."

"I don't believe you."

"I tape-recorded it," Eliot added effortlessly.

"You sneaky bastard." Sammy began to laugh. "You would have strung me along forever." He smiled and Eliot saw his face break through, pleased and honest for the first time. "I knew they couldn't touch you."

* * *

The telephone woke him up. He lay still, counting five rings before he took the extra pillow and placed it so that his head was sandwiched. He tried to move back to his dream of the hospital, the silent white rooms that had built themselves into his mind. Then the ringing started again.

"Hello."

"Eliot, I feel lonely."

"Where are you?"

"I'm in the lobby, Eliot. I had to wake the god-damned doorman to get in."

"Oh, sure," he said. "You might as well come up."

The bedside lamp had a shade of crinkled deep-purple cellophane that threw light unevenly on the sheets. Feeling like an old movie, he pulled on his white trousers and the shirt he had worn to dinner, a light blue shirt with wide white stripes. Smoking and waiting for her, he was sitting in his armchair with his bare feet shoved under the bedcovers when he finally heard her step in the hall.

She smelled of night air, cold and fresh. She came toward him and he felt within a slow, sullen click, as if that dead part of him that had used to respond to her was trying unsuccessfully to revive. Now Eliot sensed the presence of the doctor in the room, his large bald head like a light waiting to be turned on, to articulate the situation and make it go away.

"You look scared."

"I was asleep."

Lara took off her coat. Her brown eyes were large; they always seemed to grow at night, not just the pupils dilating under various influences but the eyes themselves, swelling under the humors, she used to say. Her eyes, she used to say, were her best feature, the absolute Shakespearean window to her soul, the one and only signal of the power she claimed to manipulate people, to lead them to the places she invented.

"You had a good dinner with Sammy, I hope."

"All right."

"I don't want to make things difficult." She was smiling. He wondered if she knew that since she left he had been particularly nervous at night, even frightened sometimes of the dark. Now the edges of his vision began to waver: no hallucinations, nothing spectacular, just a gradual leaking, a bleeding of the colors from the outside so gradually everything whited out.

"You're making me nervous. Don't you know how to make a person feel at home any more?"

"I'm sorry," Eliot said. "Just help yourself to anything. Have an ashtray or a drink of water." For this one moment he was beginning to wonder if this situation was taking place neither in his nind nor in the room but was a cosmological war between the doctor and Lara to see who would control him.

Two years ago his blond hair had been longer, curled down to his shoulders, and his white suits cut differently—wasp-waisted and flared at the shoulders and the ankles. He had been going down the elevator in the St. Francis Hotel, looking contentedly through the glass walls to the sparkling lights of the city. And then the police had been waiting for him, had taken him out in the warm San Francisco night, one holding a gun on him, as if he might be trained to explode, while the other emptied his pockets. But it wasn't until they undressed him, when they cut open the padded shoulders and ripped apart the seams of his wide sailor-boy cuffs, destroying Lara's careful needlework to discover a few powdered remnants of his mother's bequest, that he finally asked to phone his lawyer.

"Sure, Mr. Simon," they said. "You go right ahead. We don't want any trouble here."

"I won't give you the divorce."

"All right," Eliot said.

"Did you change your mind too? Did Sammy change your mind?"

"No. I just don't feel like fighting."

"What happened?"

He was looking at his hands. They were starting to shake but he refused to clench them, to twist them into each other, to do anything but look down and watch them flutter, indecisively.

"I came back from the station," he said.

"You came back from the station."

"They kept me there a whole month. Without anything." He

looked up from his hands to Lara, who was sitting on the edge of the bed and was in the middle of taking out a cigarette.

"I remember," Lara said. "They kept you there a whole month."

"When I came back you were living with Sammy."

"I wasn't living with him."

The room was threatening to waver. Then it stopped and all the colors came flooding back, solid and still: everything in its place. "Don't get technical," Eliot said. Speaking carefully, keeping taut the narrow walls of his voice. And then suddenly heard the sounds of his own words, not fragile at all, but harsh, almost cruel.

"All right." She had been about to light her cigarette but now she put it back in the package, stood up and drew on her coat. "I'm sorry," she said. "I didn't mean to hurt you. My baby."

She was standing in the door and he was still in his chair. She was beginning to open the door and he was studying his hands. She was framed in the yellow light of the hall. She was hesitating and then she was no longer hesitating but retreating, her footsteps blurred by the expensive hotel carpeting. He closed the door.

* * *

The morning came slow and white through the gauzy curtains. He pushed himself up on one elbow, tried to shake his head clear. The orange light of the telephone was flashing again. He looked from it to his watch, which read ten o'clock, and then from his watch to the bottle of sleeping pills his doctor had given him.

In the middle of the night, after Lara had left and he had given up on natural sleep, he had taken a pill and set out on the bureau, to encourage himself, the hotel breakfast menu. Now standing up, he saw the menu spread open. The doctor had allowed him the sleeping pills, he said, on the condition that Eliot ate. But now the menu only reminded him of the various and unsatisfactory dishes with which they might present him: gelatinous eggs, cold soggy toast, pancakes made from flour that gave you cancer—they were all the same, foreign matter that he would somehow have to ingest. Sometimes he wondered how it was that people ever ate, how they could bear to look at the food on their plates and truly imagine it inside their own bodies.

He picked up the telephone and dialed the front desk.

"This is Eliot Simon. Do you have messages?"

The voice came back, the New York vowels ripe and unexpected after his years away from the city. "Mr. Sparrow called twice: once last night and once this morning; he said he'd call back. Lara called this morning and left a message that she forgives you. Mr. Simon called this morning and asked you to call him at the home. The number is. . . ."

He had taken a shower and was dressed and drinking coffee when Sammy came to the door.

"You ready?"

"Sure," Eliot said. He was wearing his white suit again, but this day his tie was darker, a red that reminded him, as he carefully adjusted it, not exactly of blood but of the memory of blood, a nicely indirect red that might give him a tiny advantage.

"You have the tapes?"

"No. I destroyed them." With his hands clenched, his eyebrows contracted to control his face, he looked at his one-time friend and lawyer, Sammy Sparrow, looked at his new raggedy jeans and the pressed cotton shirt he had put on for this occasion, looked him up and down so slowly and diffidently, in a manner so close to the one he used to have, that for a moment he felt that things had returned to normal.

"You're making it difficult for me, Eliot. I can't guarantee results."

"You just stick with me." He reached out to tap Sammy, a parody of something he didn't quite remember, but the mornings in the gymnasium had made his body new, and he felt his fist bump solidly into Sammy's shoulder bones, knocking them both off balance.

"She'll bleed you, Eliot. Remember who you are."

* * *

He was holding the situation in his mind. The situation was getting complicated but not impossible, and for once he felt firmly established in the center. The situation was that he was in a taxi caught in uptown traffic, and beside him was his lawyer, Sammy Sparrow, his eastern wife-stealing lawyer who was dressed in his ridiculous and phony street clothes and berating him for the lie he had told about Lara agreeing to the divorce. On tape.

But although the taxi was stuck in traffic and might take another half hour to make it to the freeway that would in turn lead out of the ciy and twenty miles upstate to the nursing home where his father now lived, Eliot already felt the strain of the impending meeting. As if the old man might right now materialize onto the seedy and stained beige upholstery, point a bony accusing finger into his chest, and ask what the hell he, *Eliot Simon,* descendant of an Eliot Simon who crossed the ocean in the actual *Mayflower* and landed on Plymouth Rock without spotting the wax shine on his leather boots, was doing wasting his life pretending to recover from, of all things, his wife.

And then, suddenly, the cars broke open around them and the taxi sprung ahead. He looked out the window, saw the city shooting by, and for a moment remembered the exhilaration New York used to have for him, the crazy belief he had maintained in this junction of millions of people, billions of tons of concrete and metal all whirling about each other: deals, agreements made and broken, sudden pyramid connections when for a few seconds, from the very guts of the imperial center, everything suddenly worked and money from all over the world focused its power on one place: a piece of real estate, a mine, a chain of stores, and in that short moment transformed it, rotated the lives of everyone connected in a way that could never be undone.

"What are you thinking about?"

"My cure," Eliot said. "I think I'm getting better."

And then the traffic broke again and they were on the freeway, wheeling north. The tires hummed against the cement; Eliot let their noise enter him, soothe him, fill the new-old places that were opening up. His hands were calmly searching the package for his first cigarette of the day, and he realized that without trying he had followed the doctor's advice, his mind had switched from his father to the city, had established a screen for itself against the confrontation to come.

"Well," he said to Sammy. "Life can't be all bad." And he saw himself as if this present were already past. He saw himself as if there were some part of him already removed from this state of being, from this situation which was more than a struggle with his father about what would happen with his mother's money, more than a struggle between himself and Sammy for the affections of Lara, who in any case preferred her current Yoga instructor, more even than some dark and necessary passage in his own life; saw himself passively sitting in the back of a taxi, hands folded placidly together; saw himself wan, starting to smile, white-suited and skinny; and suddenly felt himself to be no more than an attempt by his bank balance to project someone human, an account book to live in, the living shadow of his own money.

* * *

His father was waiting for them in a room, a large room that had high narrow windows and no rugs at all on its dark hardwood floor. As they went in, Eliot put his hands in his trousers pockets and let his suit jacket fall open. It was most important not to be afraid, but it was almost as good not to seem afraid; the doctor had at least taught him about surfaces, the absolute and equal reality of his pretenses.

At first he didn't see his father. He took a deep breath, which made his chest hurt because he was so tense, and began to look again around the room, letting his eyes this time rest in the shadowed areas. It was between a dark and ornate hanging, which Eliot recognized, and one of the long glaring windows, that he finally saw him, an afghan around his shoulders, sitting huddled in a Boston rocker.

"Who the hell are you?" His father's voice, querulous and rough, drifted across the room.

"It's me, Eliot."

A silence. "Eliot?"

"It's me."

He was waiting for Sammy to go first, but finally he alone began crossing the wide floor, conscious of the sounds of his shoes echoing against the wood, of the way his jacket hung open when it should have been done up, the imperfect fall of his tie.

"I thought you were never going to come to see me." His father's voice had lost its authority, turned timid in its every sound. Eliot felt his heart, which had been thumping insistently, speed up, uncontrollably trilling as if it wanted to spit itself right out of his chest. He looked down at his father's face. Age had stained it dark, roughened the skin, made the nose arch and swell at the bridge. And his eyes, the blue money eyes he had inherited, were clogged at the corners with sleep.

"How do you like it?"

"Nice," Eliot said. "Everything looks good." The room gave less the impression of a museum than of a catalogue of what, in his own home, had become his father's obsessions: statuettes that had lived in recessed corners, paintings and hangings, valuable desks and antique chairs—all these were mixed together with worthless old books, ancient bottles of patent medicine, even favorite bits of driftwood from the beach. Everywhere he looked, there was something else, from the cornices now at the door but formerly supporting the mantel of the dining-room fireplace, to the stained glass on one of the windows, even, he suddenly realized, the very wood he was standing on.

"You moved the floor." He looked at his father and stepped back. The tone of his own voice had surprised him; it was fragile, almost submissive, but finally, because the room was swimming like a kaleidoscope burlesque of his own childhood home, admiring.

And then he felt something on his wrist. It was his father's hand on his white sleeve, drawing him closer. The cloth of his suit, he suddenly noticed, had already turned faintly gray from two days of New York air. "They'll give us some tea here." And then, in a whisper: "I told them my son would come to take me out."

"I'll get you some tea," Eliot said. His heart had frozen still. He was standing rigid, his universe held tensely in place, even his voice was solid because as he spoke he was imagining the walls in his mind, imagining them strong and firm, the long strong tunnel of his voice. He let his eyes focus on his father's, let his hands move to his father's shoulders.

"I had to get you here. They censor my mail."

"You moved the floor," Eliot said. "You stole the floor out of your own house." He felt so tense his hands were shaking on his father's shoulders, he was shaking his father's shoulders. He wanted to laugh, to cry, he couldn't breathe. He shook his father and gasped for breath, sputtering and choking until finally he had to take his hands away, push them against his chest, against his clean white shirt and his memory-of-blood tie, forcing the old air out so the new could come in. "I can't take you out," he whispered, "you're crazy." And then he was shouting, "You're crazy, YOU'RE FUCKING CRAZY."

* * *

He was coming into San Francisco on the midnight flight. The plane circled above the airport, and as it did, Eliot, alone again in the first-class section, looked down at the familiar lights, let his calm hands unfold themselves and brace against the arms of his seat as the plane tilted into its descent.

It was night. When he got off the plane, the doctor was waiting for him, sitting in the lobby as if he were a business acquaintance, even a relative.

"How did it go?"

"All right," Eliot said. He looked at the doctor but instead saw his own face—so much skin, muscle, bone; saw his face and imagined it smiling at the doctor, controlled and confident.

"It's all settled," Eliot said. "The situation is excellent."

The situation was in the center of his mind, and from there he saw himself, absolutely inspired, so false he could have flown, raise one arm and place it, loose and familiar, on the shoulder of the doctor. "It was easy. I put the muscle on him." He smiled further at the doctor and patted him reassuringly. "Let's go," he said. "It's good to be back."

BROTHERS

The sun coming up off the water is so deep and intense it could drive you crazy. At first a nice lazy craziness that lets you see how the sky holds different times of day, how the light of morning touches everything to life, how the sunset throws dark blues and reds into the corners of your mind until you no longer know if you are yourself, no longer remember what it was you were doing before you got caught. And then the craziness could become compulsory; you would no longer remember anything at all but would be so taken by the place that only it existed: the sparse grass, the dirt roads, the shacks joined by clotheslines hung with fish nets and diapers—they would become the geography of your soul, the true land from which you set out into the water and sky.

* * *

You go crazy and after a while you seem to get better. People see you have a new face, a new voice, and they think it's all been forgotten. When you seem sick it's because the hurt place makes your mind scream. The truth is you never change, you only learn to conceal it.

I've come full circle now. I live in downtown Toronto, where I lived ten years ago, and sometimes I forget exactly when it is. The thousands of times I've walked these streets full of whatever current hopes, obsessions, fears, all mix together into a curious blend that contains my whole youth.

I'm sitting at a yellow table, a table as bright and yellow as the sun sometimes was, and I'm listening to the sounds of cars moving cautiously through the snow. I've learned my lesson and now I'm cautious, too. My hair is short, my clothes fit, I have a career. But in the summer of 1968 life was perfect. Revolution, politics, electric music, strung a rainbow through my head and in their every echo I was certain I was hearing the voice of the future. History was on my side and there were no hangovers.

* * *

On clear summer mornings the sky above the harbor is a deep liquid blue stained green by the sea and yellow by the passage of the sun. It sets off the north shore, which is rock seamed by evergreens, and folds over the village on the south, making picturesque the jumble of falling-down small shacks. Along the water is a violent array of boats: skiffs, launches, sailing boats, even an old schooner with its decks ripped apart for repair. All of these are moored at docks which, with one exception, are broken by the weather. The exception is the largest dock of all, painted and straight, and it leads to a dry white boxy structure that drains away the color of the sky and is marked by a sign saying KING NEPTUNE FISH. Atop the sign, rising into the blue, is a wooden cutout man; his painted features have been obliterated by years of wind and rain, but with his vacant face he stares square at the road, his left hand on his hip and in his right a long trident.

Beyond the village proper, on a rocky promontory, is the lighthouse, and in the unprotected flats that mark the entrance to the harbor live the lighthouse keeper and his two sons. The keeper's shack is standard for the village, except that its wooden walls are reinforced by Coca Cola signs. His two middle-aged sons live in mobile homes that are permanently silver and can jab the sun's light into your eyes. They have rusted tin chimneys sticking haphazardly through their roofs and are dug into the ground to save them from the winter winds. Once, the keeper had to fire a lantern every night, but now he has nothing to do except keep the cement walls of the lighthouse painted. This he does, in white like the fish factory, so the morning first reveals these two buildings around which the life of the village moves, the two white focal points of the ellipse: the fish factory and the lighthouse.

Where I lived in that summer of 1968 was right between them, in a prefabricated cabin that sat on a hill of rock and grass that rose up like a fist from the sea. It was the cabin of a friend and I moved in there with a box of books, a typewriter, and a thousand sheets of blank paper. Every morning, I would step outside and let myself be blinded by the colors. This place was so perfect and quaint in the sunshine it needed only a postcard of itself.

Then, one morning, I woke up and the fog was pressed up tight against the window. Looking down the small hill to the harbor, I saw a whole new landscape of gray clouds rising off the ocean and wet grass. No sky. The shacks and mobile homes nothing more than oblique shadows in the gray. That morning, Hugh-John, the lighthouse keeper's eldest son, arrived carrying a box of split mill ends for the heating stove. He came curiously inside and showed me how to light the fire. Then he sat at the table and drank coffee choked with sugar and evaporated milk. We tried to look through the picture window to the sea, but the fog was only growing thicker; from an exaggerated mist it had become a viscous mass of gray and yellow.

I used to make a game of noticing people's hands. Hugh-John's were thick and covered with hundreds of tiny scars.

"Would you like to come fishing with us? We leave at dawn if the weather's good."

The next day, I woke up to the alarm at five. The fog was gone but the sky was dark and filled with ominous rolling clouds. There was a wet cold drizzle, too, and I bowed my hat into it as I walked down to the beach. Hugh-John was waiting there, sitting on his skiff, drinking coffee. With him was his brother Stanley, his greased sandy hair spiked straight up in a brush cut. Although he wasn't unfriendly, he hardly spoke to me—then or ever; words were unfamiliar. We stood on the slick dock nodding uncomfortably at each other and I felt momentarily like some exotic city lizard, skinny and useless.

The boat was powered by an old Ford engine which sat in its middle. It started easily, with an unmuffled roar, and soon we were speeding out to sea. When it slowed down, Stanley began hauling up nets from the water. Suddenly the floor of the boat was deep with silver herring. Then Hugh-John and Stanley had their knives out and were slitting open the herring and throwing the guts overboard to the crowds of waiting gulls.

In those days I hardly drank at all, but Hugh-John and Stanley were firmly stamped by the bottle. Before we left shore they had passed a flask back and forth, and now that they were cutting the fish it seemed their hands weren't quite controlled. They worked with astonishing speed but sometimes the knives would twist and flecks of their own blood would be mixed in with the herring. Then it was done; Hugh-John revved up the idling motor and we set out again. In fifteen minutes we were out of sight of the harbor.

As we traveled, the waves grew higher, until they slapped under the bow like wooden sledges. And when we stopped, the boat began to pitch and buckle. I took an oar and kept us turned into the wind while Hugh-John and Stanley baited shining steel hooks with strips of herring. The wet wind had numbed my hands and I was trying to keep them covered with the sleeves of my jacket. Hugh-John saw me doing this and offered me the gloves from his pocket.

"Don't need them," he shouted. He shoved his hands toward me, showing again the masses of tiny scars. "Can't feel a thing."

The rain increased and the sea began to calm. The brothers sat like dead logs, their arms stuck out over the side of the boat, jigging up and down. Every few minutes one of them would pull up his line and empty a cod into a wooden crate on the floor of the boat.

When we had arrived at the fishing ground I was already soaked, frozen and ready to go home. The sky, which on other days had been such a benevolent and liquescent blue, was now harsh and gray, gray as the sea, which felt colder at every moment.

Hugh-John and Stanley finished their first wooden crate and started filling a second; I fished too, not catching many because I couldn't distinguish between the weight of a fish and the weight of the line—but each cod I pulled up was applauded, and each time the line came up empty they pretended not to notice.

Part way through the third crate the rain stopped, the clouds broke up and the sun came out. We had a lunch of pork sandwiches and coffee while the day heated up.

"The weather changes," said Hugh-John. "You never know what's going to happen." Later I found out there had been two more brothers, both drowned.

In the few hours since the morning, my arms and shoulders had grown sore, my hands cut and blistered from the chafing of the line; wind and salt had baked the corners of my mouth into place. As the motor carried us safely home we passed around the flask. The warmth loosened my muscles and even Stanley's grunts and short comments seemed articulate. Closer in toward the village the water flattened out, and by the time the lighthouse was in sight we were going fast enough, throwing up long white streamers from the prow and sending spray into our own faces.

We entered a narrows and skimmed along the shore, past rows of larger skiffs and launches, until we came to the fish factory, where we moored the boat.

There had been more dead fish in this place than anyone would want to see in a lifetime, and their odor hung heavier than any fog. Pushing our dolly, we walked slowly through the almost empty barnlike structure—the last ones back—until we came to a scale at the far end of the building.

In front of it was standing a man at least six and a half feet tall. He was wearing overalls that had once been white but were now a mottled combination of blood and oil. Beneath them his chest and belly bulged aggressively forward.

Here was the real King Neptune. As in the sign, he held a long black pitchfork. But his head had not been worn away by the weather. His thick black hair glistened with oil, his dark eyes were set close together, his large fleshy face flourished with smooth features that glowed as brightly as his hair. He seemed to have been born and rooted in this place, to have been nurtured on fish oil and eggs.

He smiled as he saw us coming toward him, a close smile that showed off large white teeth. And then he set an empty wooden box on the foot of the scale. One by one our crates were lined up in front of him.

"Do good today?"

"All right," said Hugh-John.

King Neptune began working his pitchfork, plunging it into the mass of dead fish, transferring them from our boxes to his. The tines were covered with blood, eggs, pieces of scale. Sometimes an eye or a fin would be temporarily caught, then slip off with the next load. When he was done he handed Hugh-John an invoice, covered with bits of fish and scribblings.

"See you soon."

"That's right," Hugh-John said. "See you soon."

King Neptune then reached behind the scale and produced, from a metal cashbox, twenty-three dollars in crumpled bills. No more. Hugh-John creased them flat between his palms, took out a thin wallet and carefully placed the money within.

"What happened?"

"They pay five cents a pound," Hugh-John said. "They were going to raise it to seven but they didn't."

*　*　*

The afternoon was hot and muggy, the sky a shallow gray-blue that closed the heat around the harbor. I tried to sleep but couldn't, only tossed on the bed and listened to the flies that flew in squads from room to room, clustering on windows, buzzing their way to death in the dozen spiderwebs I'd neglected to sweep down. I went outside and walked along the beach, past the light-house to the open sea, where I followed the twists and turns until I came to a huge broken hull driven high up onto the sand. There was a wind off the sea but the sun seemed to burn right into me, taking root in my skin. The timbers of the hull had been smashed open and I crawled into it.

Here it was dark, hotter than the cabin, filled with the odor of seaweed. Shafts of light came in from gaps in the deck, from the doorways and shattered walls of compartments, and gradually as I made my way around I began to see bits and pieces of the ship it had once been, the remains of metal trunks, a plastic toilet seat, and finally, in the corner of a tiny room, wedged into one cranny, bones that had once been a human arm.

By the time evening came I was sitting at my cabin table looking out the prefabricated window to the sea. The sky had cleared; now its shallow blue had deepened to purple and the trees on the far shore rose into it black and jagged. With a bottle of Southern Comfort I stepped out to watch the remains of the sunset. Every few seconds, the revolving red beam of the lighthouse would pass across the hill in front of me, briefly catching me in the eyes. I was conscious of the typewriter that sat unused on the table, of the reams of blank paper that awaited. What? Perhaps only the fantasy I had had in the city, the idea that if I could just empty my mind something beautiful and necessary would come into it, perfectly formed, waiting only for me to discover it. But when I closed my eyes I only saw the bones of the dead man, wedged in tight, and I imagined him trapped by the ship's tossing, unable to swim free.

As the air cooled, it grew heavy and wet. Voices from the village carried to me, the sounds of families eating and quarreling, doors being opened and closed in houses too full for privacy. Mixed in with the sparse tough grass was a sweet clover, and now in the wet air its smell was blended with a small wind from the sea, a cool sweet smell that carried with it, gilded to its edges like tinfoil on a Valentine's heart, the dense layered gift of the fish factory.

"We'll be having a fire down on the beach." Hugh-John's voice. "You're welcome to come if you like."

The passing light caught us and in its glow I handed the bottle to Hugh-John.

"I used to live in the city. When I was in the Army."

It was so dark now there was only the shadow of the hill down to the black water. As we passed the bottle back and forth, voices rose out of the shore, the sound of splintering wood, and then there were flames jumping in the air.

When the bottle was finished, we went down and I sat on a huge rock, cross-legged, watching the fire. At its edge were Hugh-

John and Stanley, feeding it wood, raking aside coals to bury fish and potatoes. Then we were joined by their father, Hezran. He was a short man, dressed in a white shirt and flannel pants with suspenders. He was, he told me, seventy-eight years old, and his face showed every year: the skin was divided and broken, the stubble on his cheeks stood out in wiry white patches, his eyes hovered behind his thick white brows like those of animals hunted to exhaustion.

"You're from the city," he said. "My son used to live in the city." He looked at me curiously. "This was their first time out this summer. They say it's hardly worth it now."

There was a bottle of wine, and it emptied until Hezran folded his arms across his chest and began to sing old Scottish ballads in a voice so strong and tight it carried across and held the whole harbor in its net.

"You hear that," said Hugh-John. "There's no one else can sing like that." And then later: "A hundred and eleven people died. They say it was an unlucky ship."

By the time we ate, even the ache in my crossed legs was numb. But when I stood up they gave way and Hezran had to reach out to catch me. For a moment his hand dug into my arm, steadying me, then he, too, began to topple, grabbed at in turn by Stanley, who in his own time slipped and stumbled, so the three of us ended twisted and jumbled up in the sand.

Every day for a month I went fishing. All my exposed skin was roughened by the weather, my hands covered with rope burns and abrasions, my arms and shoulders swollen from hauling up the cod. But I never got used to it. When the sky was clouded over and spat rain, the cold got right to my bones and my spine still wanted to collapse. And when it was clear, the sun off the water bit into my eyes and I would see vague shapes shimmering in the smooth troughs of the waves, long for land and the darkness of my cabin. Worst of all, every day that we wheeled our pitiful crates of dead fish to King Neptune at his scales I hated him more —knowing I was trading this pain for his careless profit, to fill his huge landlocked belly and keep his black hair and close-set eyes happy and shining.

In the afternoons I would sit at my typewriter. Not to work at
my novel, which I had long forgotten, but to write detailed and
sentimental letters to my friends. I felt so taken by this place, captured, that I never went out in my car any more, never went to
Halifax or even drove around to other villages, only did my shop-
ping at the local store and bought week-old newspapers there; and
there, too, at its post office, I bought envelopes and stamps and
sent out my mawkish descriptions of the village, trying to protect
myself with words, trying to prepare for the inevitable return.

*   *   *

Now I drink a little more than I used to; some people might even
call me a drunk. I wake up early: my bones are sore, my head
hurts, my skin is as white as the bellies of fish. But despite my
own white face in the mirror, it's the nights that bother me. In the
old days I couldn't go to sleep without having lived something
through, without having completed whatever the day had begun.

One day when I came back from the fish factory I saw a rental
car parked beside my own. When I went into the cabin there was
a woman, Judith Sorrento, clutching one of my letters in her hand.
"Oh, God," she said. "What's happened?" She pulled out a tub
and started boiling water. "Everyone says you're going crazy."

"I feel fine."

"You smell awful."

Her hands dug into my back, loosening muscles that had been
knotted up for weeks. That night, I took her down to the fire at
the beach, and as the bottle came around she took her turn. When
Hezran sang she sang with him, her voice rising with his across
the harbor, rising with his first to support it but then breaking
free, cutting through the cold night air and soaring away on its
own.

The next morning, I slept in past the time of fishing and woke
to the feel of her tongue on my neck. Our legs slid together. The
sun shone hot every day. We spent hours soaking ourselves in it,
then carrying the heat back to the cabin.

Once, I woke up at dawn and went down to the beach. The skiff
was moored tight to the dock and there was no sign of fishing

gear. It was late August and the sun was slow in breaking through the mist. But as it did, the sky grew deep and moist; I could see the jagged rows of boats curving down the harbor, the fish factory rising a brilliant chalky white out of the mist. As the dawn hour passed, other boats sped out to the fishing ground, but there was no sign of Hugh-John or Stanley.

That afternoon, I took Judith down to the beach to see the wreck. We crawled in the jagged hole that had been battered open by the rocks and went from room to tiny room. Judith, more perceptive and inventive than myself, figured it all out, the function of every place and the lives that had been lived there. But when we came to the cabin with the arm bones she just stood in the door and looked at them, then moved up to touch: her fingers on the dead bones.

*   *   *

We were coming back along the beach when I first saw the smoke. It hung above the village like a big flattened question mark, lazily drifting from its own peak into a gray and diffuse cloud.

"They've probably burned our house down," I said.

"That's just the kind of thing you'd think."

When we climbed the rise behind the lighthouse, we saw our cabin was intact. But near it, where once had been a tree, was now a charred and smoking stump, surrounded by a jumble of blackened wood and metal.

As we came toward it, we saw the wide swath of burned grass; it started at the edge of the village and came within a few feet of our cabin, where it veered up the hill away from the sea. Around and in our cabin, and in the still-smoking grass, stood Hezran, his two sons, people we had never met. Seeing us, those in the cabin came outside, and as they gathered around us they were joined by others coming up from the beach and from the shacks by the water until finally we were surrounded by the whole village.

Hezran, dressed in his invariable suspendered flannels and white shirt, stepped forward. He had shaved so that his face was papery and smooth, his narrow cheeks bitten deep with lines.

"There was a fire in the grass. It was burning quick, with the wind behind it, coming up toward the cabin." He extended his long white-shirted arm, sweeping the whole face of the harbor. Everyone crowded behind him. They didn't listen to Hezran at all but only stared intently at us, especially Judith, who had been scarred by neither weather, hunger, nor even childbearing; they assessed her suspiciously, as if she were an unknowable combination of precious and evil. She smiled back at them.

"I and my sons came up here and took out the furniture, thinking at least something might be saved. We put it over there, by that tree." He pointed to the black stump. "Then, you see, the wind changed direction."

And so, of course, we could see: the sudden curve in the blackened ground. We went into the cabin. Everything was gone except the mattress; being heaviest, they had probably saved that for the last. And the table, a handmade table that was too wide for the door in any direction, also remained. My typewriter, my books, even the blank paper—all had been burned.

"I'm sorry," Hezran said.

Hugh-John walked around the inside with us. "I've got some extra chairs."

* * *

A few days later, I gave back the clothes and bedding the villagers had loaned me. I drove the green Chevrolet to Halifax, waited there while Judith returned her rental car, then drove with her back to Ontario. At night I would wake up sweating, King Neptune's face leering at me through the dark motel rooms, through the comfort of Judith's embrace.

At Christmas time a card came bearing a color photograph of the village. It had been touched up and the falling-down shacks looked like a gingerbread palace, layers of snow on their roofs and porches like so much icing. "Hugh-John and Stanley," the card was signed, but of course I never wrote them back.

COLUMBUS AND
THE FAT LADY

He moved aimlessly through the fairgrounds, letting the August sun warm him, filter through the dust and fill the gaps in his time. A tall man in his early forties, he wore a vaguely Spanish costume: tight black pants and an embroidered silk shirt. He had a sharp bearded face and large dark eyes. Despite his lack of direction he moved carefully, like a cat sensing its path. Occasionally he stopped and rubbed his hands across his ribs. They had never healed quite properly and he was aware of his body pushing out against them.

"Christopher." Rena, the Fat Lady, waved him toward her. She was sitting out behind her tent, her dress hitched up over her enormous thighs. He went and sat down beside her in a lawn chair. He took off his shirt and stretched himself out to the sun. A scar in the shape of a cross had been burnt into his chest. "Help yourself," she said, meaning the bourbon that was standing in the shadow of her chair. He drank directly from the bottle and then passed it to her. Her face was rippled like a pile of bald pink tires. "Praise the Lord," she said when she had finished. She wiped her mouth and put the bottle back on the ground. They sat and contemplated the taste of the bourbon. Christopher took another drink and passed the bottle to Rena. "Praise the Lord," she said each time she drank. And then, shaking out the last drops, "I know you're not supposed to drink in the sun." She giggled. "Yes," she said, "I surely know you're not supposed to drink in the sun. They say it makes you talk too much. At least it makes me talk too much. It makes me *want* to talk too much. Lord yes." She had a voice that was thin and husky at the same time. "Christopher," she said, "sometimes I believe you myself. Yes I do. But do you believe me?" She looked at him earnestly, across a half-empty bottle. He nodded. "Yes," she said, "it's real for sure." She took a handful of her face and shook it. "It's all real. Took me ten years." She traced out the scar on Christopher's chest. "Yes," she said, "I do believe it's real. It must have smelled something awful." Her finger had filled the gouge the iron had left. At first the scar tissue had been bright red but now it was dull and tough. He was tanned from his mornings in the sun. Felipa didn't like to come outside with him. She stayed pale and cool.

He stood up. The bourbon had made him dizzy but not drunk. "It's time," he said. He kissed her hand and put on his shirt.

"Oh," Rena said. "You have such beautiful manners." He kissed her hand again and then started on his way. He had spent months on the ocean, but he didn't have the sailor's rolling gait; he walked like an ocelot sensing its path. He waved at the candyfloss man, at the foot-long-hot-dog booth, at the man who had a new gimmick that was guaranteed to open cans in three seconds; worked his way through the games and gadgets until he came to the midway. The crowds were beginning to fill up the spaces between the tents. Some of the barkers had already started, advertising their three-breasted women, their dwarfs and talking animals. He came to his own tent and signaled to a man wearing a striped shirt and a straw hat. He was sitting on the stage with Diego, showing him how to cheat at cards.

"He learns quick," the man shouted to Christopher. Diego pocketed the cards and went to stand beside his father.

"Come on," Christopher said. "We'd better go inside." The man dusted off his pants and ground out his cigar. He cleared his throat. He spat on his hands and rubbed them together. He climbed onto the platform in front of the tent, cleared his throat once more, whistled loudly into the microphone, and began:

"Ladies and gentlemen, step right up, yes—"

On either side of the tent were large crude posters showing a trio of old-fashioned ships tossing in a storm at sea.

> "Step right up and see the world's most amazing freak of time, right here, ladies and gentlemen, come right in, only twenty-five cents, see Christópher Columbus and his ships, hear him tell about his famous voyage, see the man who found America, ladies and gentlemen, the world's strangest freak from time, see the cross they burnt onto his chest, hear about the women he left behind him, the man who met kings and princes, Christopher Columbus, only twenty-five cents, you have to see it to believe, it's absolutely true, ladies and gentlemen, bring your children, bring your friends, this is the world's only living history, hear him tell about the Santa Maria. . . ."

Water slopped across the deck of the ship, leaving flecks of foam and seaweed in its wake. Columbus was hunched into his coat, scanning the strange shore and estimating how much longer he could go without sleep. His hand moved in his pocket, seeking the familiar shape of the bottle. Fatigue had permeated him. It was like having a sliver in his nervous system. He uncorked the bottle: it wasn't working for him any more, it might have been thin wine or water. His tongue and throat were so immune it just drained down into the bowl of his stomach.

In his dream he was on land, and that, as he came to consciousness, was the first thing he was aware of. "Christopher," the boy was saying, "Christopher." He was making the name into an incantation. He opened his eyes. He was lying in a room lit by a lantern.

"Don't worry," Columbus said. He closed his eyes.

"Don't worry," a woman's voice echoed as he was falling back

to sleep. He thought again that they must be on land. He felt the
boy's lips on his hand. Tears. The water slid along the polished
surface of his skin. They had tied him to a giant wooden wheel
and were rolling him slowly through the village. When his cousin
had died on the rack, he had stayed outside all night watching
constellations slip off the edge of the earth. The priest's face was
covered with tiny pouches, his eyes gray and certain. He walked
along the Spanish coast with Columbus, one night when the
clouds were layered into prayers. Columbus knelt down on the
grass to confess. He closed his eyes and saw flesh being ground
between millstones.

"You will feel better," the priest said. "A man does not have to
carry his sins."

"Yes," Columbus said. Another cousin had been taken during a
storm. He had seen him lose his balance, start sliding across the
wet wood. He had dived flat across the deck to save him and had
cracked his ribs. Afterward, still in the rain, they had bandaged
him tightly while he drank to distance the pain. He remembered
the man's wife. She had long black hair that had crackled in his
hands.

"We only ask you to believe," the priest had said, looking point-
edly at Columbus, raising the question.

"Yes," Columbus had said. While they bandaged him, he kept
seeing the widow crossing herself over an empty grave.

The stone walls were seamed with damp lichen. They had given
him a wooden bench to sit on. From the next room he could hear
the meshings of clockwork gears mingled with the screams of
heretics. But, every morning and every evening, he knelt and
rested his head on the wood. He didn't dare use words any more.
He just closed his eyes and held Felipa in his mind. When the
image was clear, she could move around and whisper to him.

When they brought him in, the priest was there, his hands
clasped in front of his gray robe. "You will feel better," the priest
said. "A man does not have to carry his sins." Columbus nodded.
He kissed the priest's bony hands. The skin caught in his teeth
and moved around loosely.

With his compasses and sextant he had searched for God on the open sea. When he stumbled on the new world he half expected to find Him, sitting on a great carved throne, unsurprised that He had finally been discovered by mortals. The skin caught in his teeth and moved around loosely. He clamped his jaws; blood vessels popped open like grapes in his mouth.

Felipa caressed him as he slept. She drew her hands across the muscles of his back and plied his spine. Each day, the water had been different. He would stand on the deck and try to read its moods, calculate the margin of its mercy.

In his dream he was on land, and that, as he came to consciousness, was the first thing he was aware of. Felipa was holding a steaming bowl of soup out to him. He sat up and took the bowl. He smelled it and circled the strange aroma with his tongue. Diego was sitting beside the bed, watching him eat. "You hurt your elbow," Diego said. "It's all swollen up like an egg." Columbus set the soup down and slid his hand along his arm. The lump was big but not painful.

"There's a reporter here to see you," Felipa said. "She said you told her to come today."

Columbus sat up straight. They had a cot for him, backstage, for when he fainted. He could see the sun setting through the yellowed plastic window of his tent. "It's getting better," he said. "This time, I was still conscious when I hit the floor."

"No," Felipa said. "It's not good." She frowned. "The doctor said you mustn't do it any more." The reporter had come in and was taking notes.

"I can't help it." He saw the reporter. She had crouched down and was taking his picture.

"I'm going to Rena's," Diego said. "I guess I'll sleep there." He looked sadly at the reporter and his father. "I'll see you tomorrow."

"What made you decide to discover America?"

Columbus lay back on his cot and closed his eyes. "I'm sorry," Felipa said. "He's not very good at giving interviews." She stood between Columbus and the girl. The girl put away her notebook and snapped her camera into its leather case.

"I don't mind," she said. "I just wanted to meet him."

"Maybe some other time. He's very tired." She edged the reporter out of the tent. When she came back in, Columbus was brushing his hair. "Don't worry," she said. "Everything's going to be fine."

He nodded. Lying on the cot, he had suddenly been reminded of rows of men in cells waiting for time to pass. The memory made him uncomfortable. His finger traced the scar on his chest. "Is there time for a drink?"

"Yes there is. But *please,* it won't be bad tonight."

"I know," he said. "If we could just settle somewhere, I would get my bearings."

"I'm sure they're going to give you the job. The professor was very interested. He even invited us to dinner."

"I don't mind this," Columbus said.

"It's not healthy. Every time you tell the story, you faint."

That evening, they went through the usual interrogations. His heart and pulse were checked. They shone lights into his eyes and poked at his ribs. They had a tape recorder and asked him questions about the Spanish court.

When they were finished, they left Christopher and Felipa in the dining room while they retired to deliberate. Professor Andras was the first to come out. He looked puzzled.

"Well?"

"They won't hire you but they will pay you a small fee to stay on if you will let them question you. You would be welcome to live here but my wife—" he shrugged his shoulders. "I'm sorry, Mr. Columbus."

"It doesn't matter." When they were back in their hotel room, they lay on their bed in the dark listening to the breeze breathe through the curtains. He still remembered the man's wife. He had met her only once, by accident, at the edge of the forest.

"I don't want him to go," she had said. Then she had drawn him back into the trees and embraced him. "Forgive me," she had said, "make him stay." The impact of his body had snapped the railing. It had been impossible to hear him above the storm, but they had seen him fighting hopelessly in the water.

* * *

"Yes," Felipa said. "This is how it was, before." She gestured broadly, including everything in the sweep of her hand: the redwood trees, the long sandy beach, the Pacific Ocean stretching toward the Orient. Diego was already splashing and swimming in the water but Christopher and Felipa were sitting under a tree by a small stream that fed into the ocean.

"It's very beautiful," Christopher said.

"Yes."

"It seems a strange kind of ocean."

"Maybe we could sell the truck, get a job on a freighter or something."

"No," he said. "I'm tired of the sea." They stood up and walked back to the truck, to get food and their bedrolls. Rena was waiting for them there, talking with a strange girl. The girl had a camera and was taking pictures of them as they came toward her. She had arrived on a motorcycle; it was parked beside the truck. There was a dead snake beneath the rear wheel. She put down her camera and took out her notebook.

"Hello," the girl said. "I followed you."

"What do you want?"

"I want to do something different," she said. "You know, what kind of person you are, how are you with your wife and child. That kind of thing. For example, you could tell me who your favorite pop star is."

"I was born in Genoa in 1450," Columbus said. "When I was nine years old I was apprenticed to a weaver." He hadn't thought about that for a long time, the rhythms of wool and patterns, the miraculous transformation of single strands into shawls and blankets.

"What made you decide to discover America?"

Columbus sat down on the sand beside the truck and closed his eyes. "I'm sorry," Felipa said, "he's not very good at giving interviews."

"I don't mind," the girl said. "I just wanted to meet him." She put away her notebook and snapped the camera into its leather case. "I took psychology at college. Last week I interviewed a guy who thought he was Jesus Christ."

"Maybe he was."

"Oh, yes," the girl said. "I've always believed in reincarnation. My grandmother was Queen Elizabeth the First. I had to curtsy and kiss the hem of her dress every time I came into the room."

Rena had her lawn chairs and her bourbon. She pointed the bottle toward the girl and motioned her to sit down. The girl was wearing tight white shorts, rolled up as far as they would go. "Have a drink," Rena said. She handed the bottle to the girl. The girl unscrewed the cap, wiped the neck of the bottle carefully, and took a delicate sip. She coughed. "Praise the Lord," Rena said. She took a long swallow. "Praise the Lord," she said again and handed the bottle back to the girl. The girl shook her head. "Come on, it won't hurt you." The girl accepted the bottle, took another delicate sip. This time she didn't cough. "Praise the Lord," Rena said. "What's your name?"

"Laura Nimchuk," the girl said.

"I'm pleased to meet you, Laura. That's Christopher Columbus down there and this is his wife, Felipa Moniz de Perestrello. And the boy on the beach is Diego, their son. Praise the Lord." She threw the empty bottle past Laura into the back of the truck. "It took ten years," Rena said. "I never stopped eating. I had to borrow money from the bank. It was a business investment. At the end I got a contract; I had to gain fifty pounds in the last two months and it nearly killed me."

"God," the girl said.

"And it's all real, too. Here, feel it."

"I don't know," Columbus said. "I said I was going to India but all along I knew I would discover America. I guess I finally did it because I had to." The girl was stroking Rena's arm. She spread out her fingers and plowed her hands through the flesh. "It was a very hopeful thing to do. I felt we needed a new beginning." He got up and paced as he talked. "I thought there must be some place untouched by time." The girl was still discovering Rena. It was like exploring a huge geography of lukewarm spaghetti.

"It's real," Rena said. "It's not a fake at all. People used to accuse me of wearing pillows and falsies, all sorts of things. But it's all real. It was hard work, too. Don't believe what you hear about glands. I have a picture of myself when I was a girl. I was just as thin as you."

"I believe you," Laura said. "You've really accomplished something." Her hands scooped up loose flesh around a shoulder and shaped it into a vase.

"They didn't want me to go."

"I ate twenty-five apple pies in three days." They had broken him of course. He had written endless pages of confessions, lists of heresies and failures to believe.

"It's not your fault," the priest had said. "Perhaps you are possessed. I've heard of such cases." His face was covered with tiny pouches, his eyes gray and certain. "Especially since your cousin regained his faith at the end. We could try to help you, to purge you of these things."

"Or?"

"A man does not have to carry the burden of his sins," the priest said. "Not in this life." After his confessions they gave him a wooden bench to sit on. Twice a day, in the morning and the evening, Columbus knelt and rested his head on the wood. He didn't dare use words any more. From the next room he could hear the meshings of clockwork gears.

"Jelly rolls, ice cream, chocolates—they're not any good at all. The best you can do with those is get flabby. You need something that will give you a good firm base. People don't understand that. They try to put it all on at once. Bourbon and beer, they're very good for after, pass me my purse, Laura, they feed the flesh, but what you need to begin with are grains and molasses." She giggled. "I know it sounds silly about the molasses but I believe it, it sticks it all together. Feel that: it's quite firm underneath. A person doesn't want to cover themselves with goop. Like you take the lady before me, she was disgusting. Praise the Lord. She was just a slob. People don't pay good money just to see a slob. It's a science, really. Without discipline it's almost impossible to get above three hundred pounds. Of course you have to have the talent, too. I guess you're just born with it. Praise the Lord. My father taught me everything. He used to be able to put it on any part of his body at will: an arm, or a leg, or even his head. He could never get it on everywhere at once though, so he couldn't get steady work. He used to make bets with people. In one week he could double the weight of any part of his body. It's science, really, but it's not the kind of thing they teach in school, Lord, I am thirsty, getting dehydrated is the big danger, yes, feel that: it's nice and moist, I make sure to keep it that way, yes."

They had burned the cross into his chest to make sure he would carry his faith to the new world. "A man can protect himself by the sign of God upon his body," the priest had said. He had waited until Columbus regained consciousness and had gently wiped his face with cold water. It was weeks before he could move comfortably. "My own sign is chastity, but that is given to very few." He squeezed the cloth over the wound. When Columbus screamed, the priest slapped his face. "We are not trying to punish you. That is what you have to understand."

"If you want my secret in one word, I guess it was porridge."

"I don't think of myself as a hero," Columbus said. He had eaten dinner with the Queen of Spain. When she sent for him, the priest smiled, satisfied that he had had his audience first. Laura was sitting on Rena's lap. She had her notebook out again and was taking it all down in shorthand.

"Because of what happened, time doesn't exist for me," Columbus said. A tall man in his early forties, he wore a vaguely Spanish costume. He had a sharp bearded face and dark eyes. He was leaning against the truck again. "I don't know why it's real for anyone. There are always gaps, unexplained moments."

"You dream," Laura said. "At night and sometimes during the day you dream."

"I dream about my father," Rena said. "He was always changing his shape. The only part of him that stayed the same was his feet. He could never do anything with his feet. He said it saved him a fortune in shoes."

Columbus got up and went down to the beach. Diego had found some wood and had started a fire beside the stream. Felipa was there too, rinsing off clams and preparing to cook them in a cast-iron kettle. Two men had held him when they taped his ribs. He had met the man's wife only once, by accident. She hadn't wanted him to go. He had a knife and helped Felipa by prying open the clams. "Do you dream?"

"No," she said. "I just have pictures. Trees and castles and lakes and things like that. But no one ever talks. In real dreams people talk. Last night I saw a white rabbit."

"Sometimes you have to make a sacrifice," the priest had said. "It might be someone or something very close to you, something that is felt as a great loss. Or it might be something that you aren't even aware of. In such cases it can take years to discover what has been given."

"There must be something constant."

"God's love." The clams hissed as they were plunged into the boiling water. When he had dinner with the Queen he remembered his manners and didn't talk with his mouth full. But she ate carelessly, tearing the fowl apart with her fingers and throwing the remains over her shoulder.

"Yes," Rena said. "I believe everything he says, even the part about the Queen asking him to bring back souvenirs." She was washing her clams down with bourbon and whole wheat bread. The girl still had her notebook but had lost her pen. She was curled up in the firelight, her head on Rena's lap. Rena stroked her hair and played cards with Diego.

"Let's play strip poker," Diego said.

"Lord," Rena laughed. "You're too young. The sight of me would kill you." Her voice was thin but husky. "But I will if Laura does."

"Are you really his son?" Laura asked later.

"Yes."

"Really?"

"Yes." Her shorts lay on the beach, flashing in the moonlight.

"And you were with him the whole time?"

"The whole time," Diego said. He ran his tongue down the inside of her arm. The moon had laid a superhighway across the ocean.

"What was it like?"

"It was fun. But the food wasn't very good."

"I wish I'd been there." She went to the ocean and dipped her foot in the water. She stood ankle deep, looking at herself. Diego came and stood beside her. He put his arm around her. "I don't really wish I'd been there," she said. "I can hardly stand up."

"You get seasick easy?"

"I never have before."

There was noise near the fire behind them. Rena came running and tripping toward them, a blanket wrapped around her, her flesh bouncing out in all directions. "Beware the Spanish Infidels," she was shouting, "beware the Latin Lechers." She rushed up to them and dropped on her knees in front of them. "Save me, Diego," Rena cried. "Save me, I beg of you." She kissed his feet suppliantly. "Save me from your father and anything I have is yours."

"You know I can't interfere," Diego said. "I'm sorry."

"Laura, you'll help me? Please?"

"Of course I will," Laura said. She began leading Rena back toward the fire. "What happened?"

"It's too horrible."

"Now, now," Laura said. "I'll protect you." She waved good-by to Diego, the ocean, her tight white shorts, the highway to the Orient.

"Good night, Laura," Diego said.

"Good night, Diego," Rena called. "Keep your eyes on the top card."

Diego walked along the shore until he found Columbus. He was sitting on the beach, drawing maps with a stick. Diego squatted down beside him. The maps showed a clear route from Spain to India. "This is the way it should have been," Columbus said. "All the rest was a mistake."

"Yes."

"Who won your card game?"
"Rena."

* * *

He moved aimlessly through the fairgrounds, letting the sun warm him, filter through the dust and fill the gaps in his time. He had a sharp bearded face; his skin was burnished from the summer. Felipa was not with him. She stayed indoors, pale and cool, preparing for winter.

"Christopher." Rena, the Fat Lady, waved him toward her. She was sitting out behind her tent. He went and sat down beside her in the lawn chair that was beside her own, that she had placed there for him. He took off his shirt and stretched himself out to the sun. A scar in the shape of a cross had been burnt into his chest. "Help yourself," she said, meaning the bourbon that was standing between their chairs. He drank directly from the bottle and then passed it to her. "Praise the Lord," she said after she drank. She wiped her mouth and put the bottle back on the ground.

"It's warm again," he said.

"Indian summer. You could have been the first man to see an Indian." She laughed. "The first white man, I mean. It surely would have been something." She laughed again. Her face rippled like a pile of pink tires. "I guess you missed your chance."

There was a taste in his mouth that he'd never noticed before. He didn't know where it had come from. "I guess I did."

"Yes," Rena said. "You surely did pick a strange time to discover America." She tipped her bottle up high. "Praise the Lord." Laura came out of the tent. She was wearing a dressing gown and carrying a cup of coffee. She rubbed her eyes and blinked.

"Diego's just getting up too," she said. The priest used to like to bring him supper and watch him eat. He would sit beside him on the bench and watch him as he searched the soup for hidden messages. Diego was ready; he stood at the door of the tent, waiting.

"It's time," Columbus said. He kissed Rena's hand. Then he

and Diego set out together, walking around so they could come across the midway from the inside, as if by accident. The barker was waiting for them. He wore a striped shirt and a straw hat. They stood beside him for a moment, conferring about details that had been decided a hundred times, and then went inside, ready to begin.

"It's absolutely true, see the world's strangest freak from time, he's right here, yes, ladies and gentlemen, step right up here, it's absolutely true, see Christopher Columbus and his ships, hear him tell about his famous voyage, see the man who found America, ladies and gentlemen, the world's strangest freak from time, see the cross they burnt onto his chest, hear about the women he left behind him, the man who met kings and princes, yes, Christopher Columbus, and it's only twenty-five cents, you have to see it to believe it, it's absolutely true, ladies and gentlemen, bring your children, this is the world's only living history, hear him tell about the Santa Maria. . . ."

"Yes," Columbus said, "it's absolutely true." He stood on the stage in his tight black pants and embroidered silk shirt. He winked at the ladies in the audience. When the tent was jammed full the lights would go down. Felipa would come on stage, clicking castanets and singing a throaty Spanish ballad. While Columbus traced lines on the map and told his story she remained on stage, sitting on a velvet cushion. "We had sighted the coast. I had been standing on the bridge of the ship for three days, hoping for land. It hadn't rained for a week. Suddenly a great storm came up. The winds blew the ship around like a matchstick—" he gestured expansively with his hands. His voice was beginning to tremble. "And then, there was a flashing light, a clap—" His arms outstretched, his mouth open, he suddenly stopped. There was a sound like an aborted cough. His arms dropped to his sides. He fell over, unconscious. Felipa knelt beside him. She pulled a scented handkerchief from her bodice and gently stroked his head.

"And then," she said, "he was rescued. He and his son, Diego.

They were brought to my house in the middle of the night. The ship was utterly destroyed and there were no other survivors." She signaled Diego. They dragged Columbus's body off into the wings. "And now," she said, "I will sing one more song; it is the lament of a widow who has lost her husband at sea."

VOGEL

Sam Vogel carried, between his social- and medical-insurance cards, a picture of his high school graduation class. He had chanced upon it the night before he got married, and being sentimental he put it in his wallet and promised never to throw it out. In this memento he was standing in the middle of the third row, with black hair coming low on his forehead, a square almost fleshy face, round eyes. Compared to the others, he was short and unformed. Compared to himself twenty-five years later, he was almost unrecognizable. The two Sam Vogels had left in common only their dark hair, and their round child's eyes.

Because the picture was in his wallet and he had preserved it through his whole adult life, it was his first image of himself. The second, more recent, existed solely in his mind and was not something that could be seen. It was a sensation. The feel of his own body in flight, running: one foot on the ground, taking his whole weight and springing it back, while the other kicked out front, confidently reaching. And it was in the middle of such a stride, confident and exact, when his back was straight and his muscular legs were pumping, that he felt a fast and sudden gripping in his chest, and before anyone could reach him he was curled up like a baby on the special composition surface of the track.

He had been going to the health club for almost five years, starting the day Henry Weinstock took a deep breath, tapped his fingers like an accountant, and said, "Sam, your body's on a one-way trip. What are you going to do about it?"

"Get old," Sam said. "Do you want me to eat royal jelly?"

"No jelly," said his doctor. Henry Weinstock, that is, because he had started off being Henry, a friend and classmate who had stood in the back row, tall and thin, looking down skeptically on the others as if anticipating the future.

"You can start by losing weight. Every year, you come in here five pounds heavier. It's not doing you any good."

Not only did Sam go on a diet, but he also joined the Men's Health Club and learned how to jog. It took him a whole year to get under two hundred pounds, and on the same day he ran his first full mile without stopping. In that ten minutes he crossed the magic watershed; when it was over he wanted to be thin and athletic more than he wanted to put food in his mouth.

"Growing old," he said to his wife, Alison. "It's not so bad." They were lying in bed, the house uncharacteristically silent. Henry, their eldest child and the doctor's namesake, had moved out a few months before, and Marilyn, their teen-age daughter, was going through a phase of domestic bliss, sitting in her room and reading, going to sleep early.

He reached under the sheet, slid his hand to his wife's belly and squeezed it.

"Don't," Alison said.

"What's wrong?"

"I feel fat."

In the old days when she demurred, he used to rest his hand on her stomach, conjure the currents of her being, try to imagine her sexual need of him into existence. Now he took his hand away.

"You should exercise," he said. "It's great."

"I tried running. I feel like I'm falling out of my shorts."

"You could swim."

"When?"

"In the morning. Or the afternoon. Or at night. Can't you spare an hour a day?"

But his voice had already become sarcastic and she had switched off the light and rolled over to her side of the bed.

"Come on," Sam said. "We can discuss things." He waited in the silence, then felt for her shoulder.

"You discuss things. You come into bed and poke me like I was some god-damn sack of flour and then you give me your interrogation. I can't look twenty again." She turned her light back on and flung aside the blankets. She was starting to cry, tears running in the shadows around her eyes. In the old days, when he was in love with her and yearned for nothing sweeter than the knowledge that she would be his to share and protect, the changing lights of her eyes mesmerized him, a continuing proof that no one could be more real, more beautiful, more blessed by fate. "Look, for Christ's sake." Her breasts, which had once been full in his hands, now were narrow and slack, drained by the sucking of children. Her stomach rippled with folds and one side was gathered by the scar of the Caesarean that had freed Marilyn.

"So," Sam Vogel said to his wife, "you're human. You could still go swimming. You don't have to be a movie actress to put on a bathing suit."

That moment, Sam remembered: himself leaning on one elbow, other arm extended in a gesture of utmost reasonableness, voice low and calm—for once he knew that justice was on his side. And yet, when Alison again rolled away from him, he didn't object. Only thought about a magazine article that described the recommencement of the cold war, and tried to convince himself that he could overcome his craving for a cigarette.

The moment of justice lay fallow. It became a place that he returned to, an expanse of his own that he roamed and examined. Then, in a surprise maneuver, he cashed it in one afternoon on the office carpet, where he made love hastily to a girl who helped at his store, Vogel's Haberdashery. She was a third-year psychology major who was working mornings in order, she claimed, to broaden herself and gain life experience. It was the only time in twenty-two years of marriage that Sam Vogel had been unfaithful, and even during the act he regretted it, compared the joys of this smooth but unaccustomed body unfavorably with the deeper and more voluptuous motions of his wife. And catching himself with both in his mind was disgusted.

"What's wrong?" asked the girl. Her name was Emily Gathers.

"I haven't done that for a long time."

"Me neither," Emily said. But when she smiled, he felt like a newly discovered virgin.

At home, every movement of Alison's, every inflection, grated on his nerves. She seemed fat, baggy, careless of herself. He suggested drinking wine with the meal.

"What's wrong?" she asked. "Are you sick?"

"I just feel like a glass of wine. Since when are we prudes around here?"

After his third glass he looked across the table to his daughter and realized she was hardly younger than Emily, that concealed by her carelessly worn sweaters and pants was skin as sweet and desirable as Emily's, that in fact she might be offering it up to anyone, not only the boyfriends she so considerately kept away from the house, but to older men, fools like himself who were tired of their wives. And so what's wrong with that? he thought. If she wants to let herself go, why should I pay? And when dinner was finished, exhausted and unpleasantly drunk, he went to take a bath.

While he was lying in the tub, his track-hardened feet wrapped around the hot-water tap, his head resting on a towel so he could doze, Alison came in.

"Look at you," she said.

"What?"

"I can hardly recognize you."

"It's just me," Sam said.

"You look cute," Alison giggled. "You want me to soap you?"

"It's okay," Sam said. "I already did."

"Really," Alison said. In her hand she carried a glass of the red wine and it tipped with her every motion. "I wouldn't mind."

"I was just tired," Sam said. "Maybe I had too much to drink."

"It's amazing what you've done. Look at you."

"Anyone can eat less."

"Don't kid yourself. Eat less. Look at you. You've got muscles all over. Practically a boy again."

"All right," Sam said. "Don't get bitchy."

"No one's getting bitchy. I'm trying to compliment you. Can't a

wife tell her husband how handsome he is? Maybe I should send
you some flowers to get you into bed."

"You get me in bed every night," Sam said. "What are you talking about?"

But it was three whole days before Emily came into his office
again, and shut the door behind her.

"Mr. Vogel," she said.

"Don't call me Mr. Vogel."

"Sam."

"Yes, Emily. I've been wondering where you were hiding."

"I was sick, Mr. Vogel. Nothing personal. I must have caught a
flu from the rug."

"I should get it cleaned," he said. "I don't mean it to be a haz-
ard."

Emily laughed. "Mr. Vogel, don't worry about the rug. Maybe
it would be better if you got a couch."

"Don't call me Mr. Vogel."

That afternoon, she called him on the telephone and invited
him to dinner. After his running, which seemed to go more
smoothly than ever, he stood in the shower washing himself with
special care, almost able to believe that beneath the white foamed
lather lay skin deep and shining, as supple and sensuous to her
touch as hers had been to his. This despite the fact he had decided
to tell her that their relationship would be returning to normal,
and that he would promise always to be her friend and counselor,
in fact like a father, which he already was, to say nothing of a
husband who had a wife so suspicious she had not spoken to him
for three days except to call him Adonis and comment on his new
red underwear.

Showered and resolved, he followed Emily's directions to a narrow Victorian house. It was on the edge of the university area,
just a mile from his store. Walking the street and climbing the stairs
to her attic room, he was conscious of only one thing, his fear that
his son would see him or, worse, be visiting a friend at this very
house and witness his own father puffing nervously toward the
third floor, a bouquet of yellow roses furtively tucked under his
arm.

"Look!" Emily exclaimed. "Yellow for friendship. How sweet!" She put the flowers in an empty tomato-juice jar, in the center of a small table.

"Just relax," she said. "You just be still and I'll cook." The hotplate was jammed with steaming pots. Sam was so thirsty from running, he quickly drank two glasses from the bottle of wine she had set in front of him.

"I was going to tell you," Sam said. "I have a son at the university. Henry Vogel. Do you know him?"

"You told me that," Emily said. "The day you hired me. And twice a week for the first six months."

"I'm sorry."

"I myself have a father. His name is Ralph Gathers and he works for the Winters accounting firm."

"He must be proud of you," Sam said.

"He's an asshole, Mr. Vogel. That's why I moved out."

When he stood up to help her set the table, Emily, laughing, pushed him onto the bed and jumped on top of him. "Your dignity, Mr. Vogel. I love you for your dignity."

It was only on his way home that he realized he had been celebrating his birthday, his forty-fourth. When he came in the door of his house it was midnight. Alison was reading a book; the table was set with white linen, a bottle of champagne in the center, and a vase of red roses.

"I'm sorry. I should have phoned."

"You should have done something." Alison seemed composed, her face stiff and decided.

"Where's Marilyn?"

"She went out tonight. Staying at a friend's." Alison lit a cigarette, automatically offered him the pack, then retracted it. "So," she said. "What's new?"

"Nothing much."

"Maybe you were having a fire sale at the store. I know how busy it gets there."

"It does get busy," Sam said.

"Tonight you sleep in Henry's old room. Tomorrow you hear from my lawyer."

"Alison."

"Good night, Sam. Happy birthday."

She walked up the stairs. Sam walked out the door, to his car, and drove back to Emily's place. All night he lay in her bed: curled up, awake, while she enclosed his back like a warm shell, her fingers entwined in the hair on his chest, her warm breath on his neck.

In the morning, while they were drinking coffee, they sat at her small table and Sam watched the yellow light searching its way through the roses. "I can't leave my wife," he said.

"That's all right, Mr. Vogel. I have a father, too."

By now he was so open to her that the sound of her voice penetrated to his heart, her every word and breath excited him, fluttered through his blood, making him feel born again. But in his mind he knew better; and as he drove back to his store, the city streets seemed passive and complacent beneath his car, waiting for the inevitable.

He made his peace with Alison and fired Emily Gathers. They threw out their double bed and bought new, fashionable twins, each with its own bedside table and its own clock radio and alarm. He kept running around the track, four days a week after work, but it was different. His stride slowed and stiffened, and the image of himself running became almost abstract: a moment frozen out of a grainy black-and-white movie: he was the old pro now, the veteran, the man who kept running without feeling his own body, without consciousness of anything but the track jolting beneath him, his bones keeping and carrying the rhythm. And though his pace slowed, the distance he ran correspondingly increased. So by the time he was forty-six he was doing five miles, indoors in the winter and outdoors in the summer, and he felt himself running through the middle of his own life, running into darkness.

One night, late at work, he went across the street to eat supper at a delicatessen. Sitting at the next table was Emily Gathers. It took him a few seconds to recognize her. She was now polished and sophisticated. Her blond hair was long and curled onto the shoulders of an expensive suede coat. She looked entirely grown and inaccessible, but it was she who waved and smiled at him.

"Mr. Vogel," she said. "What are you doing here?"

"I have a store across the street."

"This is my friend, Janet. Janet, this is Mr. Vogel, my old boss. He has a store across the street and I used to work there until he fired me for getting the carpet dirty."

Sam blushed. And wondered if it showed on his face that it was exactly that long, two years, since he had last made love.

"Call me Sam."

"Vogel's Haberdashery," said Janet. "I used to buy my father ties there, when he was still alive."

"I'm sorry to hear that," Sam said. "We're an old store."

That night, he took Emily Gathers home. She was living in a high-rise, and once inside her apartment he had no fear of being discovered by his children. After two glasses of brandy they somehow ended up on her carpet, which was broadloom and not oriental.

"Did you miss me, Mr. Vogel?"

"Sometimes."

"I missed you, too." She sat on top of him, her legs straddling his waist, knees digging into his ribs, squeezing him as if he were a horse. Which in a way was what he felt like with her, a horse, an animal being driven to its limits. Her hands were open, palms stroking his cheeks, stroking them at first and then gently caressing them, caressing them and then slowly slapping back and forth, palms back and forth so in a lazy way he let his head nod with the force of her hands, back and forth until the blows grew stronger and each was marked by the noise of her palm against his beard, a slapping sound that gradually grew into the dull pain accompanying each blow; and then finally his head was snapping from side to side.

"For Christ's sake, Emily." He had grabbed her wrists and was holding them away.

"Didn't you like that?"

"Sure. But you know."

"I know, Mr. Vogel. I mean it's hard seeing someone after two years of not seeing them at all. On the one hand you feel as if you've always been together, familiar, you know what I mean?

But then there's another part of you, just a hiding scared part that feels, oh well, this person is a stranger. A stranger. Have you ever gone to bed with a stranger, Mr. Vogel?"

"I don't know," Sam said. "I didn't think so."

"If, for example, you went to bed with Janet. Did you ever go to bed with Janet?"

"No," Sam said. "Did you?"

"Yes."

"What was it like?"

"It was all right," said Emily Gathers. "You know what I mean. It drifted along, nothing special, and then it was over. But she didn't fire me or anything. I mean she was married but she didn't have a wife."

"You're angry," Sam said. "That's all right. Just get angry. Don't give me all this indirect bullshit." He pushed up and slid her off him, so they were both sitting naked on the rug. He looked down the slope of his belly and saw hair, grizzled and thick, ridged muscles going sideways, a waist that was defined under only a thin layer of fat. Even his arms had become shapely and defined. It was years since he had smoked a cigarette or a cigar. He hardly ever drank coffee or alcohol. In the morning he swallowed vitamins with his orange juice and at noon he ate only salad and skim milk.

"That's right," Emily said. "You're looking good. You're not dead yet, though you pretend to be. For example, you make me feel alive. Does anyone make you feel alive?"

"You do," Sam said. And it was true. Once more, her voice had pierced his defenses and his heart rode on her every word. His chest was so open to her he ached, he could feel the blood rushing through him, rushing through his chest, his limbs, the aching places in his head where she had slapped him. And for the first time in two years, he wondered what it would have been like if he had stayed curled up in her bed, her hot breath on his neck, given himself up to his own feelings.

"Do it to me."

"Don't talk like that. I'm sorry I couldn't leave my wife."

"I'm sorry I dirtied your carpet, Mr. Vogel. But look what you've done to mine."

"You're bitter," Sam said. "I should have restrained myself."

"No," said Emily. "You should have let yourself go." She stood up: slim, blond, supple—she was the exact image of herself.

"Well, Mr. Vogel. This is it."

"All right," Sam said. "I don't want to argue." He stood. His bones were sore, his loins too sweet and exhausted to care what words were being exchanged. "I was faithful to you," Sam said. "Do you know that?"

"No. But I think it's disgusting. I mean, you did stay with your wife."

"That's right," Sam said. He looked away from her and his eye was caught by a table lamp. He kept staring at it, distracted, until the glare began to hurt and join the dull ache in his face. And then, his head turned away, he was blinking: caught on the edges of his vision were small fleeting shapes: hands, feet, fingers long and curled, monkey's limbs. And, looking down at himself, Sam saw that was what he had been changing into, not a horse but a monkey, a spare and hairy monkey who was growing old, his back stooped and tired, his long arms folded across himself.

And then Emily was moving away from him and he was sitting on the couch, sorting through pants, socks, underwear, gradually getting dressed until finally he was facing her in street clothes.

"I didn't mean to get so angry. I mean it's late. You can stay here if you're afraid to go home."

"I'm not."

"Good-by, Sam. Take it easy."

He spent the night in a downtown hotel. They charged him forty-two dollars, and although he had no luggage, the porter insisted on accompanying him to the room. "Is there anything you need, sir?"

"A drink," Sam said.

"I'm sorry, sir. Room service is closed. I could try to arrange a bottle of rye."

"That's okay," Sam said.

He locked, chained, and bolted the door. With the lights off, he undressed again, afraid to see himself, and then took a bath in the darkness, washing her off him, soaping himself twice and then finally showering, standing in the dark afraid to close his eyes because he knew that when he did he would only see her leaning over him, her face close to his, her palms caressing his cheeks.

The next morning, he went straight to his store, Vogel's Haberdashery, an old-fashioned Jewish clothing store on Spadina. It was noon before Alison called.

"I worked late. I was so tired I went to sleep at the Park Plaza."

A long silence. Breath being held. Then a sigh. "You feel better? Maybe you should see the doctor."

"I'm all right."

"My brother is coming for dinner tonight, you remember. Are you planning to come home?"

"I'll be there at seven. You want me to pick up some wine?"

"Red," Alison said. "For passion."

At five o'clock Sam left the store and drove to the health club, where he began jogging his five miles. In the morning at the hotel, all day at the office, he had found himself reaching for his wallet, looking at the photo of his high school graduation class. There were things he had in common with this former self, details he could list, but whoever had lived inside that picture, whoever had walked around with whatever forgotten obsessions, had been buried in circumstance.

"So," Sam said. "What the hell! Times change. Good-by." And now, on the track, that picture began to transform itself into him running, into his strong thrusting legs, his made-over arms and forcibly narrowed waist. He could feel his own blood surging through him, a fast and sudden gripping in his chest. And it was in the middle of such a perfect stride, confident and exact, when his back was straight and his legs were pumping, that the two pictures finally melted together. And as he went down he saw himself from a great distance, as if from the skeptical eyes of Henry Weinstock or Emily Gathers. He saw himself falling, slowly, his body gradually curling, his knees moving into his chest. And felt his heart burst open.

THE HANGED MAN

They had wanted to live in the country. She was a white-skinned woman with sandy hair and a smooth uncomplicated face. His skin was darker, a deep velvet black that shone in the bright sun.

She picked the house. It was back, off the road, about half a mile away from a small village. The very first moment she saw it she laughed, a high pleasant sound that rang across the morning. The agent, who knew these symptoms, acted quickly.

"It hasn't been empty long," he said. "It's just overrun with spring." He had learned there were times to be poetic.

And besides, it was true that the lime-green grass rose impressively thick from the lawn; and the trees brushing against the white clapboard made the house seem quaintly cottage-like and rustic to their city eyes.

The house was near a small village about thirty miles north of Toronto. It was far enough away so that the air smelled green and thick and the morning sounds were of birds and wind. And it was close enough that they could stand in the yard at night and see the lights of the city stretching up into the sky, winking its secret joke at them like some giant southern eye.

In the front yard were a triangle of apple trees. She walked up to them, one after the other, burying her face in the blossoms and breathing in the fragrance as if this place alone could smell so sweet.

Inside, the house was surprisingly modern. She had told her

husband, whom she had married in England, that they should expect any house they bought to need work, that Canada was a country so recently invaded and settled that the rural areas were still under siege. Undercivilized. But in fact the house had all the amenities—from a forced-air furnace to floors that had been newly sanded and polished. There was even a large cut-glass chandelier in the front hall; with its lights on, it shone like a diamond Christmas tree.

They stood in the living room and looked out the bay window to the apple blossoms.

"The last man to live in this house was a carpenter," said the agent. "Everything is in perfect condition." He saw the woman looking hopefully at her husband. "Those old carpenters did all their work by hand," said the agent. "Nowadays they use machines." He wondered how much he should say about this carpenter. He slapped his soft palms together and paced about the floor. The metal cleats of his shoes echoed in the empty room. The couple had moved closer to the window, to the view of the pink-blossoming apple trees. The agent tiptoed silently into the kitchen. He knew there was a time when even poetry must give way to silence.

* * *

The husband's name was Ralph Emerson Kennedy. For most of his life he had been called Ralph, but his wife preferred Emerson. She said it was more dignified. "Emerson," she would say. "What do you think of having this plant here?"

By the time they had moved in, the apple blossoms were turning brittle on the lawn and the heat of the summer had begun to corrode the perfect greenness of the grass. But the old house, with its thick grout-filled walls, stayed cool on even the hottest days. The back yard had tall oak trees and a well; around the well Emerson was building elaborate trellises and arbors for the garden he could imagine five years away.

On all of the floors, except the upstairs front bedroom—which was his studio—they laid the rugs she had brought from her mother's house in England. But in his studio there was only a square of linoleum. He set up his easel in the center and stacked the half-finished canvases along the walls.

"You should paint outside, Emerson," she said. "It's nature."

"I'm not going to stand in my own back yard like a god-damned fool painting roses," said Emerson. "Or whatever they have here."

"I was just trying to suggest."

"I know." He folded her into his arms and lifted her up so her eyes were level with his.

"Emerson," she whispered. "Do you like it here?"

"Of course."

In town, in the shops, they stared at him and talked behind his back. With his black skin, his suits and white shirts, his perfectly modulated British voice, he might have been from outer space. They called him neither Ralph nor Emerson, but Mr. Kennedy. "Yes, Mr. Kennedy," "No, Mr. Kennedy,"—whatever they said in their flat and nasal voices seemed to mock him.

"You'll like Canada," Amelia had said. "It's different."

Looking at her husband's slow and usually abortive attempts to finish a canvas, she felt curious. There was something about his failure which fascinated her: it presented itself to her as a puzzle she couldn't solve. Like his name, his clothes, the way he carried himself and spoke, it radiated a pure and untouchable dignity. In his unfinished paintings, his garden which wouldn't grow, his thick books that he never quite read, he was somehow the artist and creator. Her mother had always told her that without art there was no point to money.

* * *

Every day for a month Emerson went to the village. Each time he appeared, the grocer and the woman who sold newspapers were freshly amazed; their bones would go rigid and their mouths compress. Only the postmaster accepted him. He was old, with arthritic hands. It was part of his job to sort the mail into the residents' boxes, and trying to do that made his muscles stammer, so it took a whole day to accomplish what should have been done in an hour.

One morning when Emerson went into the post office, there was a box of black puppies in the corner. The postmaster, Horace Delaney, was trying to push a reluctant finger between two letters.

"Mr. Kennedy," he said.

"Mr. Delaney," said Emerson. They had already, in previous conversations, established that though they were both named after poets, neither of them wrote poetry.

The postmaster went to the Kennedy box, took out a handful of mail, and brought it to the counter. "I'll be finished sorting in a moment," he said.

"No hurry. Nothing that can't wait until tomorrow."

"The mail's so slow these days," said Delaney. "It hardly matters any more." There was something in Horace Delaney's ruined face and abandoned eyes that reminded Emerson of crazy old men. He riffled quickly through the letters, saw they were all for Amelia, and put them in his pocket.

"Nice dogs you have there," Emerson said. "What happened to the mother?" He went over to the box and knelt down by the puppies. As he did, they squealed and whined eagerly; and when he put his hand in, one of them grabbed onto his finger and tried to suck it.

"She died," Delaney said. "They don't need her any more, they just miss her." He reached into his black-and-gray-striped vest and took out a package of cigarettes. "Smoke?"

"Thank you," said Emerson. This was part of the routine they had established, the conversation followed by the shared cigarette, sometimes two. It was a routine he liked; it helped take away the bad taste of the rest of the village. To help further, Emerson had been making in his mind an elaborate fantasy of his own village, the village where he had been born. Crazy men like the postmaster lived there, and in fact, of the people he had met in this country, only Horace Delaney could have fitted.

"You should have a dog out there," said Delaney. "Do you like dogs?"

"They're all right."

"The mother belonged to the man who used to own your house."

"The carpenter?"

"You could have called him that." The old man's fingers were curved cautiously around the cigarette. "They say she found him."

"Found him?"

"Came in the door and found him hanging from the—what do you call that thing . . . ?"

"Chandelier."

"That's it; he was hanging from the chandelier in the front hall. Even had it turned on, they say."

"Ahh."

"No one around here ever hung himself before," said the postmaster. "We all went out to see it."

"Of course."

"They cleaned it up real well, though. The agent must have shown you where they fixed the ceiling."

"No," said Emerson. "He forgot to show us that." He was trying to remember the real estate agent's face. At first only a tobacco-stained mustache and weak green eyes came back. Then the rest came into focus: receding hair, a large fleshy nose, and blotched skin soaked in years of alcoholic lunches and cheap instant food.

"No one knew why he did it," said Delaney. "He was the kind of man nothing ever bothered." All the puppies had attached themselves to Emerson's hand now, biting with their toothless mouths and squirming around like eels out of water.

"Well," said Horace Delaney. "That's the way it goes." He returned to the mail.

Emerson stayed crouched on the floor, looking at the dogs. "I guess I'll take one," he said.

"Go ahead. What isn't gone by the end of the week just gets drowned." He passed Emerson a small box from behind the counter, and an old newspaper. "Better use these to carry it home," he said. "Otherwise you'd get dirty."

* * *

He walked the whole way with one hand in the box to comfort the sleeping dog; and when he got home, and let the dog out, it immediately rolled over on its back and stuck its half-formed legs in the air. Its paws, hilariously large, were marked by bright pink pads. While examining these, Emerson heard Amelia coming down the stairs.

"What's that?"

"A dog."

"I hate dogs."

She walked into the kitchen and Emerson heard the familiar sounds of her turning on the tap to start the tea. This meant it was eleven o'clock.

The hair on the puppy's belly was silky soft. And her nipples were like tiny grains of glass. He counted six of them before Amelia came back into the room. She stood leaning in the doorway.

"A dog," she said.

"The man at the post office gave her to me."

"You didn't even ask."

"Should I?"

"No. Of course not, Emerson."

Sometimes he hated the sound of his name in her mouth. It sounded like starch and laundry soap. *Emerson.*

ToFu, she named the dog.

"Why?" asked Emerson.

"It's pure protein," she explained mysteriously. And then called out: "Here, ToFu. Come to Mummy." The dog wriggled and rolled toward her. Amelia crouched down and slapped its soft belly from side to side, then began to laugh as if she would never stop.

*   *   *

That night, they lay on their backs in bed, warmed between the heavy white linen sheets given them by Amelia's mother, and listened to ToFu's whining.

"She's lonely," Emerson said.

"She'll be all right," said Amelia. It had been her idea to lock ToFu in the kitchen. "A dog has to learn to be alone," she had said. "It gives character."

They lay in the Italian linen sheets and every few minutes shifted position, avoiding each other. ToFu's noises seemed to grow louder all the time; she was singing long piteous songs. But although he was bothered by ToFu's fear, Emerson was gradually shifting his attention to himself, to a new idea that was taking root in his mind. Already he was unwilling to face the dreams he couldn't fall asleep to, was convinced that he would see the dead carpenter swinging in his own front hall.

"We should let her up here. She could sleep in a box."

"We can't give in now," Amelia said. "It sets a bad example."

She reached for him across the empty space in the bed. Her hand felt his shoulder, hard and implacable. It always amazed her that his body was so constant. She herself seemed to fall into flabby awkwardness the moment she ate or drank too much, or if she let her exercises go for more than a couple of days. She had thought that the move would be healthy for them that way, that they would get out of doors more. But in fact it seemed that their city life had only been accentuated. She stayed inside, growing softer, and watching through the kitchen window as he did his occasional labors in the garden, his body bending easily to the earth, neither gaining nor losing from it. She slid across the sheet to kiss him. There was a long hot line where their bodies joined. Then she felt him moving away, the sudden rise of the mattress as his weight left the bed.

"I think I'll do some work," Emerson said. "I'll take ToFu with me so you can get some sleep."

"All right."

Once in his studio, Emerson began quickly. Holding the puppy under his left arm, he sketched in the picture with his right. And then stood back for a moment, matching the image in his mind with the canvas in front of him before starting to apply the paint. This time, concentration only made it grow stronger. He worked without stopping until the first light, when he went down to the kitchen for coffee, and stood by the window while the kettle boiled.

In the dawn, the garden was different than he had ever seen it. A low mist lay over the land, cutting off the view of the adjoining fields and bush, making their back yard seem as if it might be in London, as if anything or nothing might lie beyond its walls. The trellises he had partly built rose up like old ruins around the well. Flowers and hedges suggested themselves in the shadows. When his coffee was made he stepped outside with it.

The false silence of the house gave way to strange wing-sounds in the air, giant birds flying just beyond the range of his vision. He took off his shoes and socks and stood in the wet grass. In England his bare feet had always loved the feel of dew, of the fertile ground pressed against his soles. Here, they were nervous. There seemed to be a menace in the earth; through the thick wet grass he was sure he could feel the presence of winter, his own skeleton, bones exposed to the ice and wind. Then one of the birds appeared, a large blue heron with a neck like a long curving scythe. "You old bastard," said Emerson. "I'm not afraid of you today." The bird skimmed slowly by, the pulse of its wings undisturbed as their tips brushed carelessly against the oak leaves.

Emerson felt a warm pressure at his feet. The puppy had somehow waddled out from the kitchen and pressed herself against his ankles. He bent down and picked her up, her fat belly fitting perfectly into his palm. He held her in front of him so they could look into each other's eyes. The puppy's eyes were brown, with no whites showing, and deep black pupils. His own eyes, he knew, were yearly more white and less brown, and after this night would be streaked with long red rivers.

With a new cup of coffee, Emerson carried ToFu back up to the studio. He had painted the stairs, the chandelier, the rectangle of light coming in from the open door. The trick was to do it all from that low point where the carpenter's boots were as big as irons. "Look at that," he said to ToFu. But the dog had curled up in a corner and fallen instantly asleep, her head buried beneath her outsize paws. Then Emerson heard Amelia swinging out of bed, the springs' creaking followed by the sound of the bedroom door opening. He listened intently as she padded down the hall and started the bath water running. Hastily he hid the canvas in a stack of unfinished paintings, and put on the easel his project of the previous week: an abstract explosion of color.

* * *

Lying between the sheets, Emerson watched the bedroom curtains flapping with the wind. The dawn had risen gray and misty, with yellow in the sky. Now the day unfolded slowly, reluctantly, the sun choked off by clouds and rain. From the kitchen rose the noises of Amelia's breakfast, her ceaseless talking to the dog. "Come on, ToFu." "Lie down, ToFu." "Good dog." Her voice was today as flat as the voices of the villagers.

And as he lay in bed, Emerson recognized a certain feeling in himself, an uneasy sense that the smooth surface he had constructed might suddenly open up. The sensation of panic made him close his eyes; as he did, he noticed the muscles around his skull beginning to tighten. Before he had met Amelia this had happened all the time—the fear followed by panic, headaches, so much tension that he would finally go out from his room in London and drink until, relaxed and bloodied, he was ready to come home and paint for days and nights without stopping. Amelia had put an end to his depressions and fears, and to his week-long bouts of drinking, insomnia and painting. "How did you do it?" he would gratefully ask her.

"Love," she used to say. "All you needed was love."

While he went downstairs to make another pot of coffee, Emerson remembered this. In the kitchen Amelia was boiling water for her eggs. "What are you doing? Don't you want to sleep?"

"Love," he mumbled.

"I love you, too," she said. She smiled happily and put her head against his chest. "Do you want some breakfast?"

"I was going to work."

"I'll bring it up to you."

For two weeks Emerson painted in his studio all day and half of the nights. Sometimes he would take a few hours off and rush demonically through the fields, trying to exorcise the nervous tension that now possessed him. On the door of his room he installed a padlock, which he secured when he went out; and even when Amelia brought him food and coffee he was careful to make sure she couldn't see what he was painting.

Then, one afternoon, he went to the village to buy a newspaper. He found himself in the cool slatted darkness of the
magazine shop.

"Mr. Kennedy," said the woman in her unpleasant and nasal
voice. "I hardly recognized you. We thought you must have gone
away." Emerson stepped forward, reaching for a newspaper. And
she stepped back, cautious, trying not to show her fear of him.

"God-damned niggers," Emerson said. He threw the paper back
on the counter and walked out of the store. It was the middle of
August and the town was clogged with tourists. He looked up and
down the street, at the cars with their multicolored license plates,
at the children wearing their ridiculous T-shirts bearing the names
of other villages, other quaint and exciting attractions. Then he
walked back into the store. The woman was standing at the
counter again.

"Mr. Kennedy," she said. Her face was blood-red and her
hands were trembling. "I didn't mean you to take offense."

"That's fine," Emerson said. He picked up the newspaper and
folded it under his arm. For the first time in weeks his head felt
perfectly clear, and he grinned widely at the woman, enjoying her
discomfort. Then, feeling sorry for her, he placed some silver
coins on the counter. "Beautiful day," he said.

The sun and wind were warm on his skin. As he walked home,
he loosened his tie and listened to the sound of the air rushing
through the grass. When he arrived he sat down on his own front
step for the first time since they had moved there. He took off his
jacket and shirt, leaned back against the railing, and soaked in the
heat while he read. After a while he lifted his eyes and saw,
through the green leaves of the three trees in his front yard, clus-
ters of ripening apples. Amelia came out and discovered him,
half-naked, standing in the grass spitting out seeds.

"Emerson," she said. "What are you doing?"

"Have an apple," he offered.

"The dog messed my mother's rug again."

"Where is she?"

"Down the basement," said Amelia. She looked at him and saw

that his skin was beginning to shine with perspiration. "Emerson," she asked. "When are you going to show me your new painting?"

"Soon."

"Of course," she murmured, thinking how marvelous it was that he could throw himself into his work this way, understanding.

* * *

A few days later, Emerson came to fetch Amelia from the garden. She followed him upstairs and let him open the door for her. And then she saw them—five of them mounted on the walls and the last on the easel, newly completed. "Six Views of the Hanged Man," Emerson said. "That's what it's called."

She walked around the room, examining them one by one, six different views of a man hanging from a chandelier. She recognized the chandelier. It was from her own front hall, and then, looking at the different pictures, she could see other things that were the same too: the stairway, the oaken newel posts, the small window at the corner of the landing. Even the man's suit was familiar—it was the blue serge suit Emerson had worn on their wedding day, complete with regimental tie.

"Marvelous," she said softly. Every painting was done from a strange low angle; and looking from one painting to another, Amelia had the sense that the body was still turning in slow circles. The head and snapped neck were almost lost in the halo of the chandelier, but the feet were grotesquely large, could almost be smelled, inert and dead beneath the shining black leather.

"Do you think they're good?" ToFu had somehow gotten loose and was running about excitedly, skidding on the linoleum. "Tell me," he insisted.

Amelia pursed her lips and stood in the center of the room, as if she were a wealthy buyer deciding whether to purchase. "Your best," Amelia finally pronounced, in a firm, authoritative voice. "I think they're the best you've ever done." She felt as though she might be sick and had to choke back the impulse before walking toward her husband.

Emerson folded her into his arms. Then he lifted her up and waited for the hot seal of her lips against his neck.

THE TOY PILGRIM

Elmer was an unattractive child but he had a way with words. Outside of a few squeaks and burbles, he said nothing at all until the age of two. Then he began to speak in perfect sentences and paragraphs. No one was sure if Elmer's course of development was a sign of exceptional genius or of stupidity. With Elmer, despite his many accomplishments, such questions always remained valid.

Elmer was the fifth of five children and he regarded the world around him with a beatific misanthropy. Mrs. Elmer sometimes thought that Elmer's dour countenance was a reflection of his innate dissatisfaction with his position, but Mr. Elmer thought it was God marking him for having named a child after himself.

Mr. and Mrs. Elmer were religious people and went to church every Sunday without ever missing. They were kind, generous, charitable and humble. With what was left over they did their best to be loving, reverent, gracious and virtuous. To a large extent they succeeded, and, what is more, passed on their own remarkable qualities to their children. With the exception of Elmer. Although Elmer was never greedy, nasty or selfish, it was easy to see that he would like to be.

Elmer's three brothers and one sister led exemplary lives. In public school they each stood fourth in their class. In high school the girl stood tenth but the boys stood first. All the boys took law and became lawyers. One turned to stocks and bonds, a second became a professor, the third went on to politics. They prospered and participated in the order of things. The girl married a scientist and served him with unblemished perfection.

Elmer, however, was continually less than was expected of him. But there was one outstanding exception. Mr. and Mrs. Elmer were very religious people. On a Sunday morning Elmer, at the age of one and a half, was carried in his mother's arms to hear for the first time the soft harmonies of the organ. Suddenly, in the midst of one of the hymns, he let out a loud shriek and then opened his eyes and gave his mother a look of such powerful clarity that she fainted right away.

That night, she and Mr. Elmer discussed the matter at great length. Was it, they wondered, a sign of God's grace or more likely just a well-deserved reprimand? They decided to hope it wouldn't happen again, and forgot the matter.

But the minister didn't. The next day, he came around to pay a visit and inspect the child. After all, he pointed out, one shouldn't fear the unusual. If it weren't for the unusual the routine would be unbroken. Elmer, he said, was an unusual child. The Elmers agreed. That was precisely what they didn't like about Elmer. They found him unusual but not in an interesting way. In fact they found him somewhat distasteful. Of course they had felt guilty about this. But there was something about Elmer, something that made it permissible to feel distaste. Recognizing this, they ceased to feel guilty and treated Elmer just like any other distasteful child.

* * *

Being neither attractive, humorous nor generous, Elmer had a difficult time making friends and was relegated to the role of onlooker in neighborhood play. Fortunately he was lumpy and forbidding and thus escaped being made a scapegoat. His parents were acutely grateful that Elmer was spared, a fortuitous event at best, they felt, and showed their gratitude by giving birthday parties for all the neighborhood children. At these parties Elmer was silent and morose. It always seemed to be everyone else's birthday, whereas his own came but once a year.

Elmer entered public school. The family relaxed. Although Mrs. Elmer had wanted to love him and sometimes felt real warmth toward him, she found him a cold but demanding child and wondered why he had turned out that way.

In public school Elmer quickly learned how to read and was soon at the top of his class. Unlike his brothers, Elmer was notably vain about being first and seemed to lack their sense of appropriate restraint. He had become a smug and complacent six-year-old. A look of immense satisfaction lingered obscenely on his face. He also had the habit of always being the first to wave his hand in the air when a question was asked, and the teacher quickly tired of the sight of his pudgy gesticulating fingers.

Elmer's academic prominence made him the avowed enemy of the other males in the class. Consequently Elmer had to make a rather hurried exit from school. After a couple of months of his mother's asking him why he didn't stay at school longer and play with the other children, Elmer weighed the relative hostilities and formed his plan. After school one day he managed to get out ahead of the others and hide behind a tree in the schoolyard. As usual his tormentors came outside and grouped in preparation for the daily sport of chasing Elmer home. When all their backs were turned, Elmer emerged from behind the tree, lowered his head, and charged.

Before they knew what was happening, Elmer had bowled two of them over and was starting his second charge. This time he aimed at the biggest one and was himself dragged down by his target. The two of them rolled about in the gravel for a while, trying to fight, and then got tired. Elmer drew a packet of gum out of his pocket and offered everyone a stick.

When Elmer got home from school that night it was dark. His elbows and knees were scraped and his shorts were ripped. Mr. Elmer quickly surmised that Elmer had atoned for some of his sins, and although he reprimanded Elmer for being so unchristian as to fight he also made sure that Elmer got an extra piece of pie for dessert.

The next day in school, Elmer gave the wrong answer to three questions in the morning and didn't even put up his hand in the afternoon. After school Elmer hung around with his new friends for a while and then went home to his mother. She gave him a peanut butter and jelly sandwich and patted his head twice.

Elmer liked going to church. His family all sat in a row and Elmer sat at the end of the row; he had an aisle seat. He especially liked the organ music, and when the organ played Elmer would remember how, when he was very young, God had walked right inside him and become part of him. When he went to church there was always the memory of that experience and Elmer wanted it to happen again. He was pretty sure it never happened to anyone else, because no one ever said anything about it. At times he wondered if it was an ordinary occurrence and was never mentioned because it was so ordinary.

What finally convinced him it was unusual was compulsory Bible reading in public school. Elmer deduced from the Gospels that Jesus was exceptional because he had God's grace. One day he tucked the Bible under his shirt and took it home to read. He stayed up late and read all four Gospels carefully. He couldn't escape the conclusion that he, too, was God's Son and that he had some special mission to perform. The thought bothered him. He didn't want to be crucified. The Bible said that anyone who believed could go to heaven, so why should he have to be crucified to go there?

Elmer knew that he was very special in God's eyes and that he had a very special life ahead of him. One day, he knew, God would come inside of him forever and when that happened he would be God. When he thought about it, it made sense. After all, God must get tired so he probably went inside people every now and then and let them be God for a while. Elmer figured that there were probably quite a few people who had been God but only Jesus had gotten famous. That was because he had *said* he was God and for saying that he had been crucified. There was an obvious lesson and Elmer resolved never to tell anyone his secret lest the same fate befall him.

Sometimes at night Elmer would lie on his back in bed with his eyes open waiting for God to come inside him. Sometimes it would start to happen but Elmer would get scared and He would go away. This didn't worry Elmer; he knew that when the time was ripe it would all come to pass. In the meantime he had only to keep it quiet and carry on living.

There was only one person who suspected Elmer and that was the minister. Although Mr. and Mrs. Elmer had entirely forgotten the uncomfortable incident, the minister remembered it very clearly and kept his eye on Elmer when he was in church. Often, during the sermon, Elmer could see that the minister was talking directly to him as if to test him. This made Elmer uneasy and he would squirm in his seat and cough. It was essential that the minister not discover his secret: he would tell everyone and then Elmer would get crucified.

After church the minister would look Elmer straight in the eye and say, "Elmer, how are you?"

"Fine," Elmer would say. He didn't want the minister to see that he knew he was being watched, because that might give away the secret. Once, while Elmer was standing with his parents talking to the minister, Elmer was sure the minister was about to betray him. He gave Elmer a sly look and started to talk. Elmer kicked him in the shins and ran.

It worked; the minister didn't tell. Elmer was severely spanked and sent to bed without supper, but he considered the punishment minor compared to what could have happened.

After that, the minister respected the God-force in Elmer and didn't stare at him so much during sermons. Perhaps, Elmer thought, he realized that Elmer was not yet old enough to assume his eventual burdens. Or perhaps he even considered that the kick in the shins was sufficient proof that Elmer wasn't special, after all.

That was fine with Elmer. He knew that he and God could bide their time together.

After the preliminary adjustments Elmer had to make in Grade One, he had a reasonably happy existence until one night, at the age of eleven, while undressing, he noticed three darkish hairs growing near his penis. This occasioned a thorough inspection during which he found several suspicious-looking hairs on his legs and a definitely black coarse hair in his right armpit. He went into

the bathroom and looked at his sideburns. They were getting
longer. Also the mustache that he had imagined for years was
slowly becoming a reality.

Puberty meant trouble and Elmer knew it. He had read it in one
of his mother's women's magazines. Not only had he read about it
but he had seen his brothers and sister pass into it and it had
had, on each of them, a discernibly negative effect.

His sister, who had never liked him but who had at least let him
alone, had become cross with him when her turn came and had
started to criticize him for all sorts of faults, real and imaginary.
She exuded mystery and importance and withdrew her affection
from all her brothers.

To Elmer the explanation was simply a fall from grace. As far
as sexual data were concerned, Elmer had taken the precaution of
reading the relevant sections of the encyclopedia. He once remarked to his sister, who was scurrying to the bathroom with a
Kotex tucked under her blouse, that there was nothing unique
about menstruation and that she ought to accept it as the course
of nature. His sister contented herself with slapping his face and
locking the bathroom door.

* * *

During his first two years of university, Elmer's parents paid his
tuition but Elmer otherwise supported himself by working in the
summer for one of his brothers and by waiting on tables and tu-
toring high school students in the winter. At the beginning of his
third year, after his first night back waiting on tables, Elmer went
home to think. He was living in the back room of the second floor
of a rooming house.

He considered his position. Twenty years old. A third-year stu-
dent in English and Philosophy. He had no marketable talent
whatever. He picked up a magazine and started flipping through
it. He became absorbed in a short story about a young man who
sold automobiles. Then it hit him. Of course. He should have
done it years ago. First he would need a pen name. Harold. Elmer
had always wanted to be named Harold. Harold Noteworthy.

Noseworthy. Groteworth. Noteworth. Harold Noteworth. He took a pen and pad and began to write.

> The young woman raised her long curled lashes and centered her liquid eyes on the face of the handsome young man standing in front of her.
> "Oh," he said. "Hello. Haven't I met you somewhere before?"
> "You're awfully handsome," she said. "What's your name?"
> "Elmer," he said, his sensuous lips framing the word.

It was three in the morning before Elmer finished the first draft of his story. The next day, he went out and bought a secondhand typewriter for twenty-five dollars. It took him three days to type out the story. He put it in a nice brown envelope and sent it off. Then he went to the bank and opened an account under the name of Harold Noteworth. Of course, there were problems. Suppose he won the Nobel Prize for literature. Would he reveal his true name or stand by his anonymity? It was a difficult question. He should have sent in the story under his own name. But if he had done that, then he would have had to call the hero Harold. Elmer was a much more resonant name.

Having confirmed his decision, Elmer sat down to start writing his second story. He thought he could easily write a story a week. At a thousand dollars a story that would give him fifty thousand a year. Even with taxes he would be left with a fair sum. He decided to study the stock market as soon as he had some spare time.

> The ocean pounded the ragged coastline. The wind howled. It was only twenty degrees above zero. All along the shore the people waited, lanterns in hand, to see if anyone would emerge. Finally, a cry was heard above the pounding of the surf.
> "There he is," Jack shouted. "There he is and he's got her, too." The crowd heaved a collective sigh of relief and rushed out to help him in. Elmer struggled out of the

water, cradling the pale Dorothea to his chest as if to protect her from the brutal wind. When they were finally out of the reach of the arms of the sea, Elmer collapsed on the beach, exhausted by his prodigious feat. But before he passed out, Dorothea managed to press her soft lips to his ear and whisper, "Elmer, how can I ever thank you?"

The End

Elmer folded up his second story, placed it in a brown envelope, and went outside to mail it. He was incredibly tired. He decided not to write any more until he had received results from the first two stories.

Two weeks later, Elmer had his first rejection slip. But his second rejection was a personal letter saying that if he could pare down his prose the editors would pay him seventy-five dollars for his story. Elmer dutifully revised his story and mailed it back. He also put three more into production.

By Christmas Elmer had six more stories out at magazines. He also had a cardboard box full of old pocket books and newspapers to which he would refer for plot ideas and stylistic inspiration. Harold Noteworth had hit the market. Elmer deferred contemplations about the Nobel Prize and concentrated instead on growing a mustache. A certain young lady had recently been encouraging his advances and Elmer, although he had not told her anything about his enterprise, was sure his success had provided him with an enigmatic magnetism.

* * *

Elmer glided the metal nail file back and forth across his fingernails, barely caressing the adjacent skin. If anyone had walked in and asked him why he was filing his fingernails in this particularly narcissistic manner, he would have disdained to reply and returned with total concentration to his task.

He lived in a square attic room with green walls and uncomfortable radiators. Being wholly unemployed and otherwise unoccupied, he had the leisure and initiative to keep his nails in trim and clean them under the tips three times a day.

People seldom asked Elmer what it meant to be a writer. For one thing, his appearance belied his intellect. Shaggy eyebrows, low-cut straight black hair, tubby: Elmer was far from prepossessing. Nonetheless he had, as he himself was open enough to recognize, a certain stability in figure and movement, a modest lack of grace that indicated the dignified understatement which was the clearest theme of his existence.

The raindrops slid down his window. Elmer pressed his nose against the glass and peered out at the people walking up and down the street. Crisscross, their paths crisscrossed like chicken tracks, leaving no trace at all.

The sky was shiny gray, and Elmer put on his sunglasses to protect his eyes from the rainbow. He looked at the house across the street. There was a window with a drawn curtain. It had green, white and blue stripes. Behind the curtain, Helga was lying on the bed fantasizing about Elmer. She imagined him putting on his jacket and coming into her house. She wanted to hear his feet on the stairs. The thought of his bushy eyebrows was driving her insane. She wanted to go to the window and look out at Elmer. No. That would be too obvious. She relaxed and sent out mental pulses to him. The energy would arrest him in his tracks, paralyze him, drench his brain with images of desire.

Elmer took off his sunglasses; they were getting fogged. His heart beat faster. He was sure that Helga was sending signals to him from across the street. He could phone her. He thought of phoning her. He would dial her number and let it ring twice. Surely she would answer. If she didn't answer, it would mean she knew it was he and he should come right over. He remembered he hadn't changed his socks for three days. How could he go to her with dirty socks? He pulled a cardboard box from under his bed and riffled through it. No socks. Hanging from a nail on the wall was a green cotton laundry bag. It had ELMER stitched in red letters across it. Inside Elmer's laundry bag were his socks. They were all dirty.

Helga lay on her bed. Her eyes were tightly shut and there were beads of sweat on her forehead. Elmer forgot about his socks and clambered down the stairs, out the door and across the street. His knees were weak with lust as he hurled himself up the stairs of Helga's house, through the front door and finally into her room. Mad with frenzy they consummated their two-ness.

Elmer and Helga got married. The sun was a yellow disk burning up the blue sky. It was June. Helga wore a white taffeta gown and silver pumps. Elmer wore a rented tuxedo and black patent leather Wellington boots. They had cloth insteps and little cloth loops at the back to help him pull them on.

Elmer's parents came to the wedding. Everyone was surprised to see his parents. Elmer wasn't the type of person to invite his parents anywhere, least of all to his wedding. They were very uncomfortable. Mr. Elmer and Mrs. Elmer pretended to be proud, but really they were just embarrassed to be identified as the parents of someone like Elmer. They shuffled and sweated and smiled throughout. When it was over they went back to their motel and drank a bottle of rye. Then they made love for the first time in two months. Afterward Elmer's father wiped his face with his shirtsleeve and remarked that weddings were a tonic.

Helga's parents came to the wedding too. They were blond and young-looking. They paid for the wedding and rented a pastor with a modest church and a short sermon. The pastor had lanky hair and a quiet way of intoning the verities. The friends were all pleased with the modest good taste and resolved to go to church again sometime. Privately Elmer thought that the whole thing was ridiculous but he knew that Helga would feel happier. Helga felt worse. Living in sin with Elmer was fine, but she didn't think he was the type of man one would marry. Not that she had anything against Elmer, but he offended her sense of propriety. Still, Elmer would gain a sense of psychological security that he had obviously missed at home and would, when the time came, be able to pay for the divorce. He might even be good for some alimony.

After the wedding, Elmer and Helga sailed away in a wooden ship to Belgium, where they set up a shop selling yard goods and had seven blond children. Subsequently Elmer left Helga and traveled through Europe telling everyone the sad tale of his life. Seated in a dark bar at midnight, he would inflict his story on any passing stranger. Soon he became known as a bore and no one would hear him out even in a strange city. Thereafter he drank himself to sleep. When he woke up, the minister was asking him if he would take Helga as his lawful wedded wife.

"Yes," he said. It was too late to say no. It was agreed, then. They were married. Elmer was twenty-four years old. Helga was twenty-one. Her skin was white and clear and her breasts were round and firm. Beneath each breast was a fault line indicating its future course, and there was a faint wisp of blond hair just below her belly. At night she slept soundly, and when she woke in the mornings she smiled cheerfully. Her hands were nicely formed and her thighs were strong and warm. Elmer considered himself lucky to have gotten such a wife but wished she were a better cook.

He especially adored her mind. He considered it clear, pink and unbroken. In fact Helga's mind was filled with deep shadows and ruminations of which neither of them were aware. She was a latent psychopath and proved it by shoplifting a set of dishes, every Thursday. As a result of one of these episodes she ended up seeing a psychiatrist. "You have penis envy," he told her. Then he gave her a big bright red pen and sent her home. Helga ceased her shoplifting but could often be observed chewing thoughtfully at the tip of her pen.

So be it. Elmer and Helga were married unbeknownst to each other on a bright June day.

The next morning, Helga noticed that Elmer had some black hairs on his back. Had she known he had black hairs on his back, she never would have married him. She got a pair of tweezers and started to remove them. Her mother had told her, on the eve of her wedding, that marriages aren't made in heaven but have to be worked on. She had just cleared a small patch when Elmer woke up. "Shut up, Elmer," she said. "I want to squeeze your blackheads."

Elmer held his breath for twenty-four hours.

* * *

In the mornings Elmer slept late. Off their bedroom was the study, where he wrote his comic plays and the occasional detective novel. He liked to lie awake in bed in the morning and smoke cigarettes and remember his perfect writer's childhood.

In his favorite story he had been slow in school. For years he had slipped from grade to grade, always at the bottom of his class. Finally a teacher, an old spinster woman who collected china teacups, had recognized him. She had brought him to her house from school twice a week and read him extracts from Proust and Dickens. At first it had been difficult. He had squirmed in his satin chair and stretched out the cookies desperately. But slowly the innate being in him had emerged to grasp what was being offered. After two or three months he started to ask to take books home. He would read them secretly in his windowless room by the light of a tallow candle. To that first teacher he credited everything. While he was still writing short stories for women's magazines, he would go to visit her grave in the cemetery once a week. Perhaps he had even bought her a wreath with his first check.

He lay in bed unresistant to the late-morning light. Despite the money, the unlisted telephone number, the occasional recognition on the street, the two bright and well-behaved children, Elmer couldn't help but feel he had been betrayed. Why had God walked into him?

He liked to imagine that he would finally leave Helga and become a pilgrim. Walking down the street early one morning, he would feel a curious sense of release. He would feel that his whole life was at once behind him and ahead of him. He would feel that day and night had come together in him. He would walk down the street and out of the city until he came to a place by the highway where he could sit. He would be picked up by a strangely beautiful girl in an ordinary car. She would take him somewhere, somewhere far away, where he would sit under a tree and meditate. He would grow gaunt. His eyes would burn. His spine would become a conduit of energy. He would experience unspeakable suffering and profound joy. The sun would explode in an infinity of golden drops, and ten thousand buddhas would dance light and shadows across the windswept grass. There would be no reprisals.

Elmer got out of bed and looked in the mirror. His full-fleshed face was beginning to sag. There were bags under his eyes and his thick black hair was dry and lifeless.

Elmer pulled on his pants and went into the bathroom to shave.

His shoulders were sloped and rounded. He didn't like to look at them. Nor did he enjoy looking at Helga any longer. She had thickened, drooped and faded. Her blond hair was turning brown and she had the beginnings of a mustache. He remembered everything. He remembered that his sister had scurried from her bedroom to the bathroom with a Kotex tucked under her blouse. Soon Helga would be barren. He remembered that his brothers had all become successful before him. Occasionally there were family reunions: the Elmer clan gathered sleek and aging in the parental home. Wine was drunk. There were no toasts.

He went into the kitchen and poured himself a glass of orange juice. The artist, having overcome childhood disasters and obstacles, finally fulfills his innate promise. But at the very moment of his greatest success, at the exact height of his fulfillment, it is soured by the taste of truth. He realizes that he has reached the top of the hill only to face the abyss on all sides. He drinks himself to death. Or he jumps in front of a car. Or he buys an electric train. Decades of emptiness stretch ahead. Elmer plugged in the kettle and contemplated his boils.

He sat down at the kitchen table and looked out over the patio to his swimming pool. Helga had told him recently that he looked like a porpoise when he lay on the rubber raft in the swimming pool. Occasionally she still clung to him, but she had ceased to moan.

There had been a curious incident. Elmer's parents, deeply religious people, had always taken their children to church. One Sunday morning, at the age of one and a half, Elmer was carried in his mother's arms to hear for the first time the soft harmonies of the organ. Throughout the service be dozed until suddenly, in the midst of one of the hymns, he let out a loud shriek and then opened his eyes and gave his mother a look of such clarity that she fainted right away. Though the rest of his life had faded, the memory of that morning stayed with him. Elmer, seated beneath a tree in a windswept field, was finally able to draw a straight line between that fateful moment and the present. He lost himself in compassion and let his body dissolve into pure being. Elmer passed from the world.

The End

Elmer got up from the table and paced back and forth in the kitchen. In his mind he had the plot for his next comic play. It would be about a man perpetually embarrassed by himself. He looked out the kitchen window. The abyss had disappeared. It was replaced by a swimming pool. The sun exploded in an infinity of golden drops, and ten thousand buddhas danced across the surface of the water. He closed his eyes and felt that God was within him.

Helga came into the kitchen. She was carrying a basket of pomegranates. "Elmer," she said. "I didn't know you were awake."

He turned to her in the noonday light. "Yes," he said. It was as if he were seeing her for the first time. Every detail was clear to him. He took one of the fruits and bit deeply into it. He chewed the red pulp slowly, savoring its slightly acid taste. He stored the seeds in a corner of his mouth and then spat them into an ashtray.

"Elmer," she said. "How many times do I have to tell you not to be such a pig!"

JANICE

Assurance will be the means. I will walk into the room calmly, my weight well back and settled into myself. I will not notice her; she will not notice me. For a while, mutually oblivious, we will entertain ourselves with others. And then, at the exact accidental moment, we will come together, the three of us, and stand in a small triangle in the center of the room.

"How are you, Robert?" she will say. She will speak to me as if I were a friend and put her hand on my arm. Not because she wants to tell me something but because she wants him to know that she can do that, put her hand on my arm confidently, meaninglessly. "How are you, Robert?" she will say, and then she will introduce me to him: "Robert, I would like you to meet Nicholas. We are going to be married in the fall." I will nod politely and express my congratulations. Perhaps she will, to settle everything, lean forward and kiss me lightly. Not because she wants to kiss me but because she wants to kiss me in public, show affection, be meaningless and confident with an old friend who has passed out of her life.

So that is how it will be. Brief, punctuated, and stylized. Nicholas will be reassured. He will make his small talk, offer me a cigarette, and then excuse himself to get us some drinks. We will be left standing there, in the middle of the room, wearing all of our clothes. Nicholas, because he does not yet know Janice, will not hurry himself. He will stand at the bar complacently, searching out the right brand of scotch and making sure that the ice cubes are the right size for the glass. It would never occur to him that the two people standing casually in the middle of the room, wearing all of their clothes, have never before spent an entire evening doing that, wearing all of their clothes.

"How are you, Robert?" she will say.

"Fine," I will reply. I'll look down at my feet, at her feet. Her feet will look peculiar to me wrapped in their shoes and stockings. I will remember her toes sticking out from under the flowered sheets of her bed, or, even more clearly, I will remember them tanned and drying in the sun, with little specks of sand on the insteps. Perhaps I will have a cigarette. The fact that I light the cigarette with the lighter I gave her, and she returned, will seem slightly melodramatic to her. It will make her feel contemptuous of my weakness, of my need to underline the situation.

* * *

Touch football became popular, so Nicholas played water polo. He moved through the water with surprising grace. Smooth and hairless. One couldn't help thinking that he might have been injected with silicone. "Isn't he good," Janice said. She had moved close to me so that our thighs ran side by side.

"Oh, yes," I agreed. "Excellent. It would be a pity to marry a man who couldn't swim." Nicholas stood at the edge of the pool, a towel draped around his shoulders. He was a beer advertisement who resembled a large Adonis. He was looking up at us, his face open and wet.

"They've decided it's half-time," Janice said. "Come down with me and talk to him." She stood up. My pants were glued to my leg by a thin line of sweat. She walked away from the bench where we had been sitting, walked over to Nicholas. Later, in the boathouse, she stripped off her jersey as if it were the most natural thing in the world, as if there were a social convention prohibiting jerseys in the boathouse. "Wait a minute," she said. She reached into her bag and pulled out a bikini top. "Well," she said when we were seated in the boat, "we can't just sit here."

"It's so hot in the sun," I said. "It would be so much cooler to stay here. We could take off all our clothes and make love in the rowboat."

She tried to smile at me but the smile slid down into her chin. She pushed the dock gently so that the boat was set in motion, gliding out of the shadows into the lake.

"Why did you come?"

"Why did you ask me?"

"It was Nicholas's idea. He said you looked so depressed at the party. He thought, you know, it might take you a while to get used to things."

I rowed out into the lake and across to a place where there were no cottages. There was a path leading up from the water to a little plateau. Lying on our stomachs, we could barely see the heads bobbing up and down in the pool that had been built a few yards away from the lake. "It's just the same," she said.

"It always is."

"Why did you come?"

"I wanted to."

She giggled. "What would Nicholas think?"

"Nicholas has drowned. Didn't anyone tell you?"

* * *

"Nicholas is very clever with his hands," Janice said. Nicholas was standing in the middle of the room, a glass in each hand, juggling ice cubes.

"Perhaps he ran away with a circus."

"You should be grateful. Not everyone would be as understanding as Nicholas." She slipped her hand into my arm and extracted a ligament. "Look," she said, "now you've spilled your drink. I'll have to get you another one."

Nicholas had worked his way from two to three to four ice cubes. People were standing in a circle around him, clapping in time to the clicking of the ice against the glass. When he had all four ice cubes going well Nicholas sent the glasses into the air after them so that the room was filled with his act. Then he caught the glasses again and all the ice cubes clattered home, still cold and intact. I was disappointed. I had wondered if he could juggle water.

He went over and joined Janice at the bar. He put his hand on her shoulder and gave her a kiss. Later he will think how lucky he is that he has found someone like Janice, someone with intelligence and beauty bound together by an inner grace. He will ask himself again why she was attracted particularly to him and then will remember, anticipate, her passion with him, her praise of his strength. He will think that it is not only his special virtue that has brought them together but that there is something else—a fatedness, a chemistry, a unique bond that exists between them on some level more profound than words. Complacently, gratefully, he will turn out the lights and slide into bed with her. Now he was only talking to her. She nodded in agreement and came back to where she had left me. "It's time to go," she said. "Nicholas will wait for us in the car."

"Nicholas is very understanding."

She moved her hand over my face as if she thought that I had turned into a panda bear with a wet nose. "Come on," she said, "we haven't got all night."

*　*　*

"Don't worry," he said. "I won't hurt you." He moved around the ring easily, flicking his hand out occasionally, not making contact but pointing to the places where I had left myself open. He had insisted that I learn to box. It would improve my confidence. He assured me that athletics had made him over completely. "I used to be like you," he said. I was going for his nose and teeth. I would feint a punch to the body and then hit him in the face as hard as I could. Nicholas would move his arm lightly and brush away the punches. "You're trying too hard," he said. "Relax." I leaned against the ropes, wondering if I would bring up. Then we started again. I used the same strategy, feinting toward the stomach and then going for the face. His ribs were so well covered with flesh and muscle it was hard to know exactly where his diaphragm was. There is a place that is unprotected. When the pattern was nicely established, the feint and the punch, I estimated where it was and accomplished my revenge. "That's better," he said. "You're getting better all the time."

Standing in the shower, I could feel the blisters on my feet raw against the tile. Nicholas, all friendliness, slapped me on the shoulder. "How about a swim?" he said. "The pool is very clean."

* * *

My shoulder was so sore I could hardly raise my arm. Janice knelt over me, tenderly licking it. "You see," she said, "when you're angry the only person you hurt is yourself."

"You're getting as bad as Nicholas."

"Nicholas thinks you don't like him."

"Nicholas is getting nervous."

"Nicholas is perfectly relaxed about everything."

"That's good. I think I'm getting an ulcer."

"Poor baby," she said. "Let Momma kiss your tummy."

"Why don't you marry me?"

"I'm marrying Nicholas."

"What for?"

"If we were married would you let me see Nicholas?"

"No."

"What would you do if I saw him anyway?"

"I don't know," I said. "I guess I'd leave you."

"How touching!"

* * *

We spent one summer in a cabin near a lake. There was no electricity, so we went to bed early every night, sleeping on a porch that faced the sunrise. In the morning I would wake up to see the light lying flat and pink across our bodies. When I turned to her she was always awake. Not just waiting but lying there awake, as if she had no need of sleep or as if she had made the transition from night to day as easily and gradually as a cat. We would walk down to the lake in that early-morning light, the grass still bright green with dew. And after we swam she would lie on the beach soaking up the sun, her body so still that when she got up the imprint was perfectly defined.

One night when I couldn't sleep, I woke her up and asked her to marry me. I don't know why I asked her, perhaps it was because everything between us had been flawless. Perhaps it was because I was curious. She didn't answer me. She got out of bed and went outside. I sat up, lit a cigarette, and imagined being married to her. I will remember her as a series of images: her hair brushing against my shoulder, her eyes opening to me as I drink to her marriage, her tanned wet summer thighs. If we had lived together we would have had a room with a skylight. Our days and nights would have passed almost unnoticed. Our bodies would have stretched beyond our skins and ended in some galaxy that we never knew. If we had lived together we would have thought ourselves gods. It was at least possible.

"Robert," she said. "Do you still want to marry me?"

"No."

There was half a moon. Enough for us to see each other sitting in the grass, watching the stars. She turned her head toward me and opened her eyes wide so I could look into them. I saw nothing. She might have been a witch. She might have been an ordinary woman sitting naked and beautiful under the late-night summer sky.

* * *

Nicholas stood beside me on the balcony of his apartment. He smelled faintly of expensive cologne and toothpaste. "Robert," he said. He shifted his weight from one foot to the other, waiting for the opening. "Janice wanted me to ask you something . . . a favor. It isn't necessary, you understand . . . but I would like it too. . . . It would be a kind of gesture. . . ." He put his hand on my shoulder and looked at me directly, man to man. "We would like you to be the best man at our wedding."

"I would be delighted."

"Good," Nicholas said. "We hoped you would." He took his hand away and we turned again to face the city. He looked happy. It was the first time I had ever seen him look happy. "You know, Robert, when I look out at the city, sometimes I wonder if everything is as it seems."

"Yes. There is always that question."

"No," he said, "I don't think you could know what I mean. You're too caught up in your own . . ." he wanted the exact word, the knockout punch, "unreality."

"I should have been a poet."

"No. You should have been a lawyer." He tugged his forelock. "Of course no one is perfect." Janice came out and joined us. "He's agreed," Nicholas said. "Isn't that wonderful?"

* * *

"How are you, Robert?" she will say. She will speak to me as if I were a friend and she will put her hand on my arm. It will be after the ceremony; we will be standing outside the church waiting for the cars to come and take us to the reception. "Did you notice the way the priest looked at us? He must have known everything." She will laugh.

"When are you leaving?"

"Not until tomorrow. We will want to wait a day, spend the first night here. I'm sure Nicholas will get drunk." Then she will squeeze my arm, turn to me, and kiss me lightly. Not because she wants to kiss me but because she wants to kiss me in public on the day of her wedding, show affection, be meaningless and confident with an old friend who has passed out of her life. "You will be here when we get back."

"Yes." All I will have to remember is to say yes to everything she asks, as if anything else were out of the question, as if it were bad manners to wear a jersey in a boathouse. Eventually they will find me, but by then time will have intervened, turned us into old friends who were once intimate.

For the last time, on their wedding night, Nicholas will ask Janice about me. She will be standing in the kitchen of their apartment, naked, making orange juice for the morning. "Robert? I never could have married someone like Robert." She will take a long-stemmed rose and put it in the empty champagne bottle, in the center of the kitchen table. Then she will walk into the bedroom and lie down on the bed. He will hear what she has said but he will not really hear it. The note of dismissal and finality in her voice will close the subject for him. He will think it is not only his special virtue that has brought them together but that there is something else—a fatedness, a chemistry, a unique bond that exists between them on some level more profound than words. Complacently, gratefully, he will turn out the lights and slide into bed with her.

* * *

When I woke up, the first thing I did was to look at the alarm. Ten o'clock. I got up and went straight for a cigarette. The place looked terrible. There was an ashtray dumped upside down in the bedroom. In the living room everything was as it had been left when the last person went home. There were glasses all over the place, ashes, butts and stains on the carpet. I went into the kitchen. Janice was sitting drinking coffee and staring out the window down at the parking lot.

"You look awful," she said.

"I feel it." I went and poured myself a glass of orange juice. "Who was that idiot juggling ice cubes in the living room?"

"Nicholas someone."

I finished the orange juice and started on the coffee. "Where did he come from?"

"He's staying with the people down the hall." She laughed. "I've forgotten their names too." She stood up and came over to me. "You *do* look awful." She kissed me lightly on the lips. She slid her hand into my arm and extracted a ligament. "Look," she said, "you've spilled half your coffee. I'll get you another cup, no, you get it, I think there's someone at the door."

* * *

They were playing water polo. Nicholas moved through the water determined but graceful. "Isn't he good," Janice said. She had moved close to me so that our thighs ran side by side.

"Oh, yes," I agreed. "Excellent." Nicholas was resting at the edge of the pool. He was looking at us, his face open and wet.

"Let's go upstairs," Janice said.

"Here?"

"Why not? No one will mind."

Later, lying on the bed, we could hear the shouts and splashing from the pool. "You know," Janice said, "I like making love this way, unexpectedly."

"I saw you sneaking off with Nicholas."

"Don't be silly," she said. "I only do that with strangers."

GLASS EYES
AND CHICKENS

On a certain summer morning, Mark Frank followed his daily habit by taking out his glass eye, inspecting it, then wiping it clean with dew. He then replaced it and, with his bare feet set firmly in the cold wet grass, relieved the night's pressure from his bladder. He was a short stocky man with a wide back, a welder by trade, a man who habitually lifted heavy iron and tanks; and although his muscles ran heavy and his gut hung out over his wide leather belt, he was still strong enough.

But the glass eye was the first thing anyone would notice about Mark Frank: like his other eye, it was brown, but because it had been a bargain twenty-five years ago, the white had aged into porcelain yellow and the brown had turned beige with the sun. He had a square, muscular face, his love of order showing through the square set of his bones, and meeting him for the first time it was hard to know which eye suited him better—the dry light one that stared at you without moving, or the moist dark one that kept blinking, too nervous for the man who carried it.

On this summer morning, he had already looked into his twin brother's room and seen it was empty. This he noted carefully, as he did everything else. He was the elder by two hours, and somehow it had become known to him that keeping track of things was his task. For this purpose he had recently bought from the Salem drugstore a set of orange scribblers: they were now hidden in his closet, though the first was almost filled. This idea of keeping a record had occurred to him when a nearby widow told him of the excitement of finding her daughter's diaries; now he thought warmly of his own, and their subject, which was the growing craziness of his twin brother, Pat. His most recent entry had been almost hopeless:

> Tonight I saw him spend five minutes staring at a potato. Ever since he got that job he doesn't eat right. He told me he thinks his brain is shrinking and I also say it is. After he finished looking at his potato he said he couldn't eat it. I ate it for him. He spent the whole night trying to tell me about his brain. I told him to go to a doctor but he said it wouldn't help. He has a map of a brain on the wall of his room but I say he won't find himself there.

In the time of his father's sobriety, there had been a white frame farmhouse surrounded by four barns, two hundred acres of only mildly rocky land, and a huge maple bush that backed down to the lake. Successive waves of alcoholism and fire had swallowed the land and burned down the original house. The new house was only the old pig barn in disguise; it was flanked by the two other remaining barns, which sat in front of it like twin warnings of disaster. Between them, leading from the house to the highway, was a hundred-yard driveway littered on either side with dead vehicles and spare parts, a true cornucopia of ancient and rusting cars and trucks. They filled the barnyard better than pigs or cows ever had. Like crops, they were planted from time to time and harvested when needed; but unlike crops, they demanded nothing, had no rhythm of their own, only the rhythm of his own days and whims.

He was standing on the grass in his bare feet, his plaid shirt tucked into his large and baggy pants, when he heard the beginnings of a muffler-less truck a mile away down the road. He listened and he blinked. Blinked once and blinked again. The truck, he now knew, belonged to Randy Blair. Every day, its noise had been getting worse and now it was the worst it could get.

He went into the house and set down his empty cup. He was never conscious of looking out one eye rather than the other, but the world was always wider on one side, so as he brushed his hair in the mirror above the sink, he tilted and craned, trying to be sure he had gotten the part straight. It was wasted effort: his hair was so thin and so well trained he could have made the part by running his hand once over his scalp. By the time he went outside, the truck had arrived and Randy Blair was walking across the grass with his young half sister, Lynn Malone.

"Guh-day," Randy said. He slurred the words together. Tall and big-boned, still fleshy in an adolescent way, blond-haired and fair-skinned, he seemed from a different planet than his own half sister. She was skinny, and her dark hair was parted in the middle, but it was her eyes that were exceptional: wide-set, deep brown and large, they were like an adult's eyes in a child's face, eyes exactly like the three real eyes of the Frank twins.

"How're you doing?" Mark Frank asked. Then, "Who you got here?" to Lynn.

Lynn nodded. She loved the sound of Mark Frank's voice; it was like rusty iron being driven together. "Talk some more."

"Go on," said Mark, grabbing at her.

She danced away. "You know what?"

"No."

"I made fried eggs this morning for Mom and Pat. I broke open the eggs and I landed them in the pan." Telling this, Lynn remembered the sound of the egg hissing as it struck the hot pan, the thick transparent fluid turning white, setting and fixing itself just as fast as she could watch.

"Well," Mark said. "I hope they didn't die of it."

"They did," Lynn said, thinking he meant the eggs. "They died of frying."

"You're a killer," Mark said. "I should take you fishing."

"You should." She saw Mark Frank's arms coming out for her and danced away again. She was wearing canvas shoes, because her mother said the iron could cut your foot and make your blood go bad, but now, feeling good to be out of the truck, she kicked them off and stamped her bare feet into the grass. "Pat made me promise to feed the chickens."

"Then you better."

"I want to watch you fix the truck."

"You come back when you're done." This last pronounced by Randy, in a voice that told her she had been pigging for attention.

She picked her shoes up and moved off through the yard to the back of the old barn where the chickens lived. The bits of chrome and mirrors shone through the air brighter than any flowers, and when she came to the place where the chickens lived, in the lee of a gigantic yellow junked grader, she climbed up into the driver's seat and let the sun and its reflections from the metal roast her warm.

The chickens, which were always being forgotten, came up to join her, scratching and gabbling until they were all around, their wings fluttering and their necks jerking convulsively in the hope of food. "What do you want?" she asked, knowing. "Do you want to be fried?" They cocked their heads at her. "Do you want to be boiled, fried, baked, or eaten raw?" The chickens, six of them, began to hop about her, sometimes brushing her with their feathers. She reached out and grabbed one by its ankles, holding it out at arm's length and trying to look at its eyes. They were tiny, tiny black eyes circled with red, and they seemed to look out one to each side. In her palms the chicken's legs felt like wet skinny sticks. When the bird struggled in her grip she held it tighter, afraid and fascinated, the feeling of its movements jumping through her. "Settle down," she said, trying to imitate her grandmother's voice. "Come on, now, settle down, settle down." The bird twisted and then opened its wings and tried to fly. Its legs bunched up in her hands, and for a moment she felt dizzy, felt that the bird was going to have a surge of strength and tow her up into the air. She let go and the chicken fluttered a few inches, then collapsed in her lap, scuttled across her bare legs and fell off the grader to the ground, where it lay on its side.

Lynn climbed down slowly. Its head was still moving in pecking motions but it didn't seem to be trying to get up. Although she had grabbed it before, now she was too frightened to go close.

"Come on," she said. "You have to get up." The bird looked at her through one of its sideways eyes. For some reason Lynn became convinced it was trying to cry. She had never looked right into the eye of a chicken, but now she did. It glittered, so tiny and shallow it seemed there could be no brain behind it. "Come on," Lynn said. "You have to stand up straight." She went to the doorway of the barn and took out a tin of grain, which she mostly scattered on the ground. The five healthy chickens began pecking so quickly at it they might have been having fits. But the sixth lay still, its head moving slowly, the rest of its body frozen.

"Come on," Lynn said. "Here's something to eat." She put a few grains in front of its beak. "Stand up now. Stand up and have something to eat." The bird didn't seem to notice. She decided to overwhelm it with the smell, and she dumped the rest of the tin on the ground so there was a small mound of grain and seeds in front of the chicken. But it didn't move.

"I'll help you," Lynn said. She stepped forward. She didn't want to touch it again, could already feel it turning on her as soon as she got close enough, trying to peck out her eyes. "Come on," she ed. "You know I'm sorry. I'm very sorry. I didn't mean to hurt you."

Then she slowly reached out her hands, putting one on top of the chicken's exposed wing, sliding the other under it, between dirt and feathers. As she did, her hand seemed to catch, pushing the feathers against the grain, and the chicken shuddered at her touch. "Come on," Lynn said, "I won't hurt you."

She lifted it up and set it on its feet. She held it out from her, as far away as she could, its beak twisted off to one side. "Stand up. Stay standing so you can eat." She withdrew her hands. It tried to flutter its wings—one worked but the other just jerked spastically, and the imbalance made it fall over again. Immediately, this time less afraid, Lynn reached out for it: her fingers dovetailed into the feathers and she could feel its heart battering against her palms as she set it on its feet again, right in front of the mound of grain. Hesitantly, it bent down to eat. Without looking back, Lynn turned and started to run.

When she got out front again, Randy had already driven the

truck over the welding pit. Without asking, she slid down under the bumper and joined Mark Frank. The sudden dark was like a blanket over her eyes; she had to close them, and when she did her field of vision filled with the image of the chicken, a white cloud of feathers hobbling about its pile of grain, then collapsing, dying, and ready to be found lying in a small white circle, head tucked underneath, ready to be turned over and inspected, to be confirmed dead in the suddenly immobile neck and dusty eyes.

The sizzle of the welding torch was like the sound the eggs had made when they hit the hot metal pan. She looked at Mark. In his welding goggles, standing on a wooden box to be close to the tailpipe and his teeth bared in concentration, he was like a stout wide-necked fish reaching for the surface. From one end of his torch a long blue-white pencil of flame reached out to the rusted metal, making a circular shower of red sparks around Mark Frank's head. From the other end extended two rubber hoses, oxygen and acetylene, that led out to the twin tanks strapped together on the dolly that Randy was holding still. Lying at the side of the pit was the old muffler, and the attachments for the new—which Mark Frank was trying to weld to the old tailpipe.

A fish, that was what Mark Frank looked like; he looked like a fish because he hunted them and then Lynn thought she must look like a chicken, a dark-skinned, dark-meat chicken.

"I hurt one of the chickens," she said. "It fell off the grader."

She saw Mark Frank stop and turn off the torch. Then push up his goggles. Welding always made his face sweat, so when he took the goggles away the skin around his eyes was white and coated with small drops of water.

"I couldn't help it," Lynn said.

"Help what?"

"The chicken. I hurt a chicken." Now she saw her brother crouched down at the edge of the pit, glaring at her while Mark Frank rubbed his face and tried to catch up with the conversation.

"God-damn tailpipe," Mark Frank finally said. "It's so rusty it can't be joined again." The pit where Mark Frank worked, welding the various undersides that were brought to him, was completely dark except for the perimeter of light that seeped in under the edges of the truck, and the glow of a grease-covered light bulb. This bulb, with a wire hooked under one axle, made the belly of Randy Blair's truck look like the insides of a person: long tubes and shadows implied a vast tangled network of iron, and looking at it Lynn felt vaguely afraid, as if it might be sick.

"I think it broke its wing," she said. "The chicken that fell off the grader."

Mark Frank came closer to her. In this light his eyes seemed both the same, only the one that was real needed to be rubbed and blinked every few seconds. "Hey," he said. He reached out for her, and this time she let his big hands fall on her shoulders. "We better go back and see."

"All right."

Randy started up the truck and moved it so they could climb up to the ground. She watched Mark go first, his flannel shirt had come untucked and leaning forward it hiked up to show his back, fat and hairy like a bear's. She had seen Pat's back too; it wasn't hairy at all, though her mother said they were twins. Then she followed him up the ladder, her bare feet testing each rung carefully, convinced the strain he put on it might have made it unsafe for her.

In the sun she saw that her arms had gotten so cold they were covered with goose bumps. She slapped at them with her hands, walking with Mark and Randy through the heaps of iron to where the grader stood. In the night she had woken up twice to hear Pat and her mother talking. Usually they sounded as if they were trying to drive the bed right through the floor, but last night had been quiet, whispering, the sounds of secrets being passed back and forth. She didn't like secrets, secrets that were hidden from her or secrets that she had to keep to herself: like this chicken she was sure they would find dead, keeled over where she had left it, and even as they came up to the rusting yellow grader she knew it was too late. She had wanted Mark Frank to find it while it was still alive, so it wouldn't be her fault when it died.

But when they reached the machine there was no sign: a small pile of grain remained, what she had dumped out, but there was no body. Over near the barn door a group of chickens shoved and pecked in their convulsive way, but going near them Lynn couldn't tell if any of them was her chicken, the one that had been hurt. "It must be somewhere else," she said. "It must have hid in here." She looked under the grader, around the machines, in the shadowy door of the big barn. And as if this was what he did every day, Mark Frank looked with her, getting down on his knees to peer under rusty cars that had been parked for decades, slowly walking the circle around the grader, trying to search out any place the chicken might be.

It was Lynn who found it. "Here," she called. "Over here." She had in fact started to believe it wasn't hurt after all, and that the worst that was going to happen was Randy's anger. And then, standing beside an old green Chevrolet, trying to warm herself in the sun reflected off the broken windshield, she had just happened to look inside. And to see, huddled in the corner of the green velour-covered seat, a white chicken, shrunken down into a perfect white ball, its feathers tucked closely around itself as if it intended to die by disappearing.

But its neck was stuck straight up into the air and its eyes were wide open, staring one to each side. "It's okay," Randy said. He opened the back door and reached for it. As he did, it toppled onto the ground, completely stiff, and lay with its legs sticking out one way and its head the other.

"Well," said Mark. "It's only a chicken."

"Are you going to eat it?"

"No."

She watched him as he went and got a spade from the barn. The goose bumps from her arms wouldn't go away and she had to keep slapping them warm as he dug the hole and put the chicken in it. Then he made her shovel the dirt back on top. With every motion, she was afraid she was going to slip into the hole after it, and when she was done she was afraid the dirt would collapse on her if she stamped it down.

"It's okay," Mark said. He lifted the shovel high in the air and pounded the surface flat. "It could have been any chicken. It might not have been the one you thought."

"It was."

"You don't know."

"Yes I do." She stared up at him. With his welding goggles pushed back on his hair and his glass eye almost transparent in the sun, he looked more like a fish than ever, a big old fish that no one would ever be able to catch. She let him put his arms around her and lift her up in the air. Randy had moved away and was picking his way back to the truck. Mark smelled like grease and sweat and fish guts.

"Do you want to cry?"

"No. But you can carry me."

As they walked back to the truck he bounced her up and down, up and down, it seemed he had been doing this forever, that she could always remember being in his arms and being jounced like a baby against his chest. And he carried her down into the pit again, let her stand beside him as the truck rolled back into place and he held the torch up to it again.

She stood beside him, her hand clutching his pocket. He smiled down at her, then pulled the goggles over his eyes.

"All right," Randy shouted, as if there were a great noise to be overcome.

"All right."

The taps from the welding tanks were opened. Mark took out a match and held it to the nozzle. There was a loud pop, then the blue flame leapt out and Mark Frank pressed it to the metal, sending sparks in a perfect red circle around the seam. Lynn closed her eyes. The sizzling metal sent her back to breakfast, to the eggs dying in the pan, then back to the night before, the sounds of secret whispers. Now she had her secret too; she could feel it folding up in her mind, the feel of her fingers plying white feathers and bones, she could feel it folding up in her mind and finding a place to hide that would be covered in white feathers and dust.

A man finds out his own brother is crazy and he begins to wonder about himself. Who knows what could happen to a person who is taking care of someone whose brain is growing smaller. He is lying in the next room to me and the same blood runs through us. I breathe his air. I dream his dreams.

And as she dozed, Mark Frank could feel her sleeping weight grow heavy against his leg. He shifted his foot to prop her up, then squinted closer to where the flame touched the metal. It was growing red, red and redder. Then finally the metal gave way and ran together.

COUNTRY MUSIC

There was an old lady who lived near a dump. The old lady got tired of looking out her window at the dump, so she spent two whole summers cleaning it up and planting flowers on top. I was driving down the road one day and where there used to be a dump I saw a garden. I got out and went over to look at it. There were plastic flowers, and from close up you could see the edges of rusted tin cans growing out of the soil.

The old lady waved at me from her window, so I went in and had a cup of tea with her. Yes, the old lady said, I guess those Frank brothers are pretty crazy. They take after their father, Old John MacRae. He was even crazier but he only showed it once or twice. Once was right after the war, he had come back to live with us on the family farm even though he wasn't wanted. One day he got so mad he ate a half a sack of potatoes. Wasn't sick either. Best appetite and biggest belly in the history of the township. He said he would finish the sack but he wanted to leave himself something for dinner. Then he walked out of the house and wasn't seen for a week. He was my own brother, too. I don't even know if I wanted him to come back. He did, though. Came back and finished off the potatoes.

Patrick Frank used to drive his old Ford truck into town every Wednesday afternoon to buy groceries and hang around the hardware store. He liked to shoot a game of pool there, but they closed the hall after Joe Canning tried to set fire to the owner. He walked in with a can of kerosene, poured it over Mr. Liston, and lit it. Now Mr. Liston builds cottages for tourists and owns the drugstore. Joe Canning is in jail for setting fire to a barn. Patrick Frank is parked in a field forever. He wanted to buy one of the tables after the pool hall closed but they were sold, all at once, to someone from Toronto.

Patrick Frank's twin brother, Mark, is known to be the crazier of the two. Once, he got so drunk lying in the hot summer sun that he passed out on the side of the road. Pat Frank and Billy Clenning saw him there, so they went and got a can of black rust-proofing paint, some deluxe off-white wall enamel that was in the barn and an old roll of wallpaper and took off all his clothes and decorated him. Mark Frank was so drunk that when he woke up he didn't even realize what had happened until he tried to pull down his wallpaper to have a crap. But that wasn't the incident that made everyone think he was crazy.

Driving out from town, along the road that goes to town, you come to a place where there are a whole bunch of little roads going out from the main road. The little roads lead to cottages and farms. At the place where the big road starts turning into little roads is a general store. Since the turn of the century, the store has been burned five times and gone through a dozen owners, but right now it is a lucrative business in the summer. People around here are terrible liars, one woman told me. When Mark Frank found he had been decorated he was so happy that he went to the store to show it off to everyone. A retired engineer and his wife from Florida were buying baked beans and maple syrup when in walked Mark Frank wearing nothing but paint and a strip of wallpaper down his backside.

Howdy, folks, said Mark. One false move and I'll shoot you dead.

You meet some crazy people where you least expect them, and sometimes it makes you wonder how they got that way. And of all the crazy people in the county it was agreed that Pat and Mark Frank were the craziest. Welfare drunks, that's what they were, welfare drunks. Pat Frank was tall and fleshless as a desert runner. He played fiddle at all the parties for thirty years. Held it against his chest and made up songs to go with it.

I was leaning against an old half-ton truck, watching Mark
Frank cut through another half-ton truck with a welding torch.
There wasn't just one half-ton truck, or two, there were more than
I could count. Saved them for tires, he said, for tires and trailers
like the one he was making me by cutting off the box of a truck
that hadn't moved for twenty years. He was sober all that summer, so he said, at least while his brother was in the hospital.
Used to play the fiddle like no one you ever heard, always had a
smart answer for anything you might say. When he picked him up
off the floor to take him to the car you couldn't believe how light
he was. The man had disappeared from drinking.

People out here are terrible liars. That's what one woman told
me. We were sitting on her front porch and she was telling me
lies. Now she's married to a prosperous farmer, but once she was
known to be going out with Mark Frank. After he turned into his
true self, which anyone could have predicted, she used to get
teased about how she almost married him. I can see you now, her
husband would say, you'd be drinking and singing away just like
the rest of them. I bet you wish you married him instead of me.

And every time he says that, she blushes and says well who was
that floozy you used to take to the movies. I guess you only
needed one when she gave you what you wanted.

And every time she says that he just grins and slaps the table.
Now, you know that isn't true, he says. I never bothered taking
her to the movies.

People out here are terrible liars, the woman said to me. You
can't trust a thing they say. Now, that old lady, the one up the
road, she's an aunt to the Frank twins and she told them that their
father would have married the widow Frank if he hadn't been
crazy. Why, he only went and saw her because he was in a state of
shock. It was his unconscious mind that made him do it. When he
realized what he had done he got out of there so fast you couldn't
have believed it.

What's this unconscious mind stuff?

It's what a person has in his head that he doesn't know. Like
the way a cow always goes for a garden.

When Pat Frank got out of the hospital he would have killed

himself if he hadn't passed out first. A man can't drink too much when he's been in bed for two months. You have to get used to it. Mark Frank and I were passing a wine bottle back and forth in his junkyard. Now, people like you, he said, you come out to the country but you see things through city eyes.

I don't know, I said, right now I can hardly see a thing.

That's right, he said. Only good thing to be said for you is that you know it.

I bought the wine, I said.

But the bottle was empty. He threw it through the windshield of an old Chevrolet that had been waiting for it these past fifteen years. Never mind, he said. He reached into his shirt and pulled out a mickey. Now you look over at that house there and what do you see?

What house? All I could see was a bump in the field.

That's my mother's house, he said. Stood there for fifty years without moving. Burned down two winters ago. Only problem is, he said, hogging the bottle, you can't live in it now.

Tell me about your aunt, I said.

The old lady?

Yeah.

I don't know, he said, there isn't anything to tell. Only see her once a year at Christmas. If the snow's not too bad.

What does she do all day?

I don't know, he said. Listens to the telephone. Can't make a phone call without her breathing down your neck. I tell her to get off the line but it doesn't do any good.

The old lady who lived by the dump had been married to a man named Tom Gorman. No one remembered anything at all about him except two things. The first gets told about three times a month: one time when a shed was burning he picked up a two-hundred-pound pig under each arm and carried them to the house. The remarkable thing about this was that the man was lame. The second thing, which people have forgotten about, is that he hated John MacRae, his wife's own brother, one-time lover of the widow Frank and father of the craziest twins in the county. And because the old lady is the widow of the man who hated their father, the twins only visit her once a year and not even that if the snow's deep.

This and more Billy Clenning, comrade in arms of the Frank brothers, told me as we sat by the lake sampling his homemade wine. Right from where we sat we could see the old sugarhouse that John MacRae had built, the only thing he ever did in his life except spend a night with the widow Frank.

Billy Clenning's father and lame Tom Gorman had been pretty good friends. Especially good friends in a place where people never get too close. To celebrate their friendship and the spring every year they boiled down some maple syrup. They would sit and drink and keep the fire going for a couple of weeks. It made them enough syrup and sugar to carry them through the year and sell a bit besides.

There are places you can walk, pockets and valleys, where you can't see any signs of the last fifty years: no hydro poles or metal fences, not even roads except for old ruts that might have been gouged by a wagon. So that's what it was like when John MacRae decided, after ten years in the war and in the city—from here the two are almost the same—to make his return to the old home-stead. In that ten years he had never sent any communication at all. He showed up, in his fashion, one Sunday at church—dressed up in city clothes and sporting a mustache. There is a picture of him in his fancy clothes and mustache in the old lady's kitchen. She pointed it out to me one day when we were playing cards. He is sitting on top of an old pine hutch in a gilded frame, posed in a rocking chair with one leg crossed perfectly over the other, his leather shoes gleaming. They must have dragged the chair out onto the lawn so there would be enough light. Bits and pieces of the house are in the background. And I also noticed, to tell the truth, that the old lady cheated even though we were only playing for a cent a point.

Everyone was glad to see John MacRae when he arrived at the church. Afterward, he and his suitcase got driven over to his sister's farm. Maybe they even took the picture that day. In the picture he is trying to look like a country squire on a mission of mercy.

At first things went pretty well. He and Tom Gorman never got to be friends but John MacRae was healthy enough to work and though he didn't do much he came in handy. He was still young, only thirty-two, and he let it be known that he had a little money in the bank and was just waiting around deciding where to buy.

John MacRae was what you could call a slow man. He had waited ten years to come back to the farm and after a while it looked like he might wait another ten before he got married and bought a place of his own. In the meantime he enjoyed himself. He did a few chores and he ate his sister's cooking. He constructed a huge sugarhouse to replace the old one that Tom Gorman and Billy Clenning's father had been using. Maple sugar, he said, was like money in the bank. There was nothing you could sell like maple sugar.

Down the road lived the widow Frank. She was just a bit older than John MacRae and it was thought that eventually he and she would see what was necessary and get together. The only person standing in the way was the young daughter of the widow Frank. About seventeen years old and pretty, she started to come visiting the Gorman farm. Not exactly officially, but you could tell it was John MacRae she was after. He wasn't too old for her: he had city clothes and he had seen the world. Maybe she thought he would elope with her. Two years passed. John MacRae put on some weight and lost some teeth. His city clothes wore out and he didn't change his overalls from one week to the next. The pretty young Frank girl from down the road visited less often. She got married and moved away. He visited her mother, the widow Frank, a couple of times but his heart wasn't in it.

To console himself he ate. With everything he ate he had maple syrup or maple sugar. Pretty soon he was all stomach and hardly any teeth at all. His mustache grew wild and caught in his mouth when he was chewing. He spent so long over dinner that he hardly had time for an afternoon nap. The widow Frank told one of her neighbors that he was getting disgusting before his time, and that, as far as she was concerned, she didn't care if she never saw him again.

When the widow Frank announced that she was through with

John MacRae, she destroyed Tom Gorman's last hope for peace in his own house. He was so mad that if he hadn't been lame he would have kicked John MacRae from the house to the road. Not only was John MacRae eating twice as much as any normal man but he was teaching the children bad habits and driving his wife crazy.

This and more Billy Clenning told me as we moved on to the second bottle of the historic recipe. Of course people around here are terrible liars, the woman said. They've lied so much they've forgotten the truth. One time, Pat Frank was at a wedding eating everything in sight. Someone asked him to play the fiddle. Well, he'd forgotten it. It's invisible, he said. Then for the rest of the day he walked around making noises like a bullfrog and trying to sing through his nose. Even to this day he won't admit he forgot it.

And that time she was telling me the truth, because I asked Pat Frank about it one day after he came home from the hospital. Oh, no, he said, I didn't forget it. It had shrunk up and I had it in my pocket. He coughed. He was so thin, his cheeks had collapsed completely. He wasn't the same man at all, Mark said. No point trying to stop him drinking now.

Winters are always long in the country, but John MacRae's last winter there was long indeed. When the weather's bad you are cooped up in the house, and when it's good there's so much to do you can hardly enjoy it. In the morning, again at noon, then from dark until bedtime the family was in the kitchen. Probably John MacRae's picture was up on the wall even then. What must he have thought, looking at it? Perhaps he never bothered.

If the snow hadn't melted early they might not have been able to get into the bush to make syrup. But by March it was almost gone. Early that month John MacRae, glad to be out of the house and away from Tom Gorman, went out and tapped the trees: bored the holes in the bark and set in the narrow metal spiles. The weather stayed good and Tom Gorman and Billy Clenning's father went and got everything ready for boiling down the sap. The very most important step was to bring enough homemade wine to last the two men at least three weeks. During their annual drunk they cemented their friendship, prepared for the long summer ahead, and fed the fire inside the huge arch John MacRae had bought for the sugarhouse.

In those five unwanted years, John MacRae had learned at least one thing. He had learned to stay out of the way when the serious drinking began. His job was to organize the kids, Billy Clenning included, into carrying the sap to the storage tank and splitting the wood. And while John MacRae stayed out of sight, the two men, after spending a couple of days plotting to throw him out in the spring, forgot him and passed on to more pleasant topics. They even, and Billy Clenning heard them, said they might let him hang around another summer if he could be got to do a little work. After all, he had built the big new sugarhouse and even if he was lying about the nest egg, they were doing okay selling maple syrup every season. In fact, they admitted, they made more than twice as much as they ever had before the new house was built. And so it went. The women did what they had to and let the men be and the kids sneaked in whenever they could to watch their fathers drink and swear.

One day, near the end, when the men had run out of wine and were roaming about, the old lady and John MacRae were in the sugarhouse alone. They were finishing off a batch of syrup and the sap was boiling away thick and hot. Suddenly there was the loudest scream you ever heard, and the old lady, young then and John MacRae's sister, came running out of the shack shouting that Uncle John had fallen into the evaporator pan.

Well, Billy says, by the time he got there Uncle John was rolling around in the snow trying to get cooled off. When he stood up, all the syrup had turned to taffy, and Billy says he was the most amazing thing he ever saw. A big fat man standing up with a thousand strands of taffy coming out of everywhere and stretching, like a huge tent, right to the ground.

As it turned out, he survived. Tom Gorman and Billy Clenning's father cut the taffy off him with their pocketknives, and what the kids and dogs couldn't eat they broke into small pieces and sold that summer at the church bazaar. He couldn't walk, they had to hitch up the horses and drag him home. Though he was badly burned he only complained once: that was when they cut off his mustache. A few weeks later he was better and except that he had turned a bit crazy, you wouldn't have known that it had taken two strong men four hours to cut him loose from his cocoon. But the experience had unstrung him. Fat and ugly as he was, he walked down the road one April day and proposed to the widow Frank right on her front steps. She invited him in, one thing led to another, and when he came out they were married by God and engaged by intent. But, like I said, John MacRae had turned a bit crazy. After a couple of days of being engaged he must have forgotten it had happened, because the last anyone saw of him he was heading down the road at six o'clock in the morning, carrying his old suitcase and wearing his city suit. Whatever he'd come for he'd got.

In due course the twins were born. The widow Frank gave them her first husband's name and admitted that she was just as glad John MacRae had disappeared and, as far as she was concerned, she didn't care if she never saw him again.

People around here are awful liars, the woman said. Now, someone sooner or later is going to tell you that when John MacRae came out of the sugarhouse he said his own sister had pushed him in. He probably fell in drunk. Still, she said wistfully, you should have seen him when he came out. Just a big mountain of taffy, I guess he looked good enough to eat.

How do you know?

I was there, she said. I used to sneak around after Billy Clenning.

In the fall, Pat Frank died. After the funeral, Mark Frank and I sat down in the cemetery to do whatever you do after a funeral. I wonder if you see anything when you're dead, he said.

I don't know. Right now I can hardly see a thing.

All you city people are the same.

Your nose is too long.

It is?

It's too long for the rest of your face. If it was a little longer it would be noble; if it was a little shorter it would fit in with the rest. But as it is, it's hopeless.

I never noticed it.

That's because you're cross-eyed.

You know what? he said. You're right. I'm cross-eyed from looking at my nose that's too long. I never knew it. How long do you think this has been going on?

It was the first thing I noticed.

And you never said anything?

No.

Soon we'll all be dead.

Soon enough.

Me, the old lady and Pat. There won't be anybody left at all.

No.

If old MacRae hadn't of been so crazy we'd have been dead long ago.

You wouldn't have been born.

He arced the bottle into the gravestone that had been waiting for that very moment, waiting for almost a century. It had been waiting so long it was half toppled over and eaten away by doubt. The bottle crumpled against it and made a neat pile of glass. You know the old lady? he said. If I wasn't so dumb I would have killed her years ago.

THE UNIVERSAL
MIRACLE

In the winter of his thirty-seventh year, Harvey Zackman woke up early in the mornings. Through the leaded panes of his bedroom window he would look out at the gray-yellow sky and his mind would fix on his grandfather, who lay less than a mile away in the Princess Margaret Hospital For Cancer. Louis Zackman was there for treatments; every week he was brought to a lead-insulated, plastic-covered cone which bombarded his chest with radioactive particles. Every day, Louis's wife, Dorothy, telephoned her only grandson and asked why he wouldn't visit at the hospital.

"I don't know" was all Harvey could say.

"It wouldn't kill you."

"I'm sorry. I'll see him when he comes home."

"When he comes home."

The thought of his grandfather's illness always pushed Harvey out of bed and down the two narrow flights of stairs to his kitchen, where he would set water boiling for coffee. All night long, there gathered a tension just beneath the surface of his skin, and by morning he could sense black focal points creating themselves, galvanic nodes of fear and betrayal that would eventually become tumors.

"Don't be stupid," he would say to himself. "I'll see him when he gets home."

At least this was what he said during November and December. He was living alone in a renovated town house bought with the profits of his legal practice. During the past few years he had watched himself grow from a dilettante into a solid citizen, but now his grandfather's plague was turning his private castle into a shell for his insomnia.

In January his refusal began to waver; each morning while the coffee filtered he thought that such a visit might actually be possible, that this might be the very day to brave the hospital. Sarah Chernik, who was his partner in legal and other matters, grew bored with the sight of Harvey sputtering nervously through the mornings.

"Just go," she said. "Just call a taxi and deliver yourself there. It wouldn't be so bad."

"I can't."

"It's stupid to fight with him now. You should have done it years ago."

"I'm not fighting with him."

"Then, why can't you go?"

In February they gave up on Harvey's grandfather and drove him home in an ambulance. Within hours Harvey arrived.

"Look at you," Louis said.

"What?"

"You've been losing weight. You look terrible. What's wrong?"

Louis Zackman had always been, even in his old age, a strong and powerful man. Now Harvey saw before him a skinny red-necked loose-skinned imitation. His voice had been burned out by freak neutrons, and stray particles had loosed the colors from his eyes.

"You look great," Harvey said. "Do you remember The Miracle?"

"Sure," said Louis. "I could still do it."

They were speaking of a device that would clean automobile oil so efficiently that the oil would never have to be changed. It was conceived during the Great Depression and at the time was named by Zackman The Universal Miracle, in a soft reverent voice he could conjure for it alone, right to the end of his long life. Even in the summer before he had gone to the hospital, Louis Zackman had sat in front of his color television, with the drapes open, and said that as far as the energy crisis was concerned, he had always known it would happen. Although it might not have, had the miracle been brought to its final conclusion.

His own final conclusion took place in the afternoon, in March. Harvey was sitting in his office when Dorothy telephoned him the news.

"He's dead."

"Who's dead?"

"Don't be a smart aleck," Dorothy said. "I'm talking about your grandfather."

"Where is he?"

"He's sitting right here and he's not going anywhere."

At the funeral, surrounded by his entire clan, Harvey felt as if the identity he had spent half his life constructing had been canceled out. Short and almost squat, the Zackman men all looked alike with their dark coats and big round heads. Only varying degrees of graying and baldness distinguished one from another.

"In my opinion," said Stanley Zackman, Harvey's father and Louis's only son, "he could have done it any time." Although Louis Zackman had spent whole years of evenings pouring oil through everything from rusted screening to shredded silk, it was well known that his failure to achieve the miracle was due to Dorothy's last-minute skepticism.

In the perfect reverse of poetic justice, Dorothy Zackman, at eighty-eight, had outlived her husband and was his chief mourner. Her hair had been specially coifed, which meant it was an almost iridescent blue, and she had surrounded her thin goiterish neck with the diamond necklace Louis Zackman gave her when he retired from business for the second time.

On the same occasion, he had paid for three plots in a mid-Toronto graveyard which had been bought by the city's Jews when such land was worthless. Now it was surrounded on all sides by tall apartment buildings, and taxes had gotten so high there was no money to administer the grounds. The yard's lack of trees was accented by the raw wind, and it had all the charm of a deserted parking lot.

In his will Zackman had stated that he wished to be buried in the old orthodox manner. Although distant Zackmans died regularly, they had themselves disposed of, in Louis's opinion, like Christians, so in this case no one, not even his son Stanley, knew what to expect.

"He's a bit of a sport," Louis once said, trying to explain him. "I mean he's a mutant. I mean you don't have to worry, you won't turn out to be your father."

"I like my father," Harvey said.

"We all like your father."

The truth was that Stanley was foolish. He didn't drool or expose himself, but he could sit for whole days reading the paper and drinking tea. Stanley's wife and Harvey's mother, Bella, was an Italian Catholic who was ostracized by the rest of the family. She boiled water for Stanley's tea, practiced her devotions, which she had promised not to communicate to Harvey, and ran the store while Stanley studied the comics. When Harvey was twelve, Bella died and Louis came downtown to inspect the accounts.

"Not bad."

The store was a secondhand-furniture operation on Queen Street East, deep in the Toronto tenderloin. "Good sturdy junk," Bella used to call it: wooden dressers, chrome kitchen tables with matching chairs, hide-a-beds upholstered in speckle-threaded silver and gold, were the stock in trade. And at the periphery, which grew in from the edges of the store and lapped in waves over the center, were thousands of auxiliary wares—from the world's largest assortment of old waffle irons to the complete bridal suite of a bankrupt hotel, including a bed reputedly slept in by the king of England himself.

"It's a mess," Louis said. He had wandered with Harvey around the crowded shop. Every movement threatened to start an avalanche. Near the back, buried under a stack of green plastic lampshades, he found a safe. And after a few days of prodding, Stanley came up with the combination. Shortly after this, Louis and Dorothy moved into a larger more suburban house, and Harvey began working at the store after school, helping Louis, who used this excuse to come out of his first retirement.

"After all," Louis said, "we might as well sell this stuff as give it away."

At this time he was sixty-seven years old. He had large arms and shoulders, which he claimed were developed by chopping wood for a dollar a cord when he immigrated, short muscular legs, and a head which was shiny on top but sprouted two bushy white wings of hair. Unlike his son, he was no sport. He worked all the time, and when his spirits lifted with the soaring sales of the store, he remembered his old project.

"Harvey," Louis asked, "what are they doing to cars these days?"

"I don't know."

"I'll tell you. They're wearing them out. And do you know why? They get grit on their insides. A car using dirty oil is like a person eating ground glass. What do you think of that?"

"I don't know," Harvey said. That night, he started having dreams of his stomach bleeding from the inside.

The next day, Louis cornered him again. "Have you ever heard of a perpetual motion machine? It goes all the time and it always stays new. Science can do anything."

* * *

When Louis Zackman died it was Harvey who had to call the funeral home. He looked it up in the business directory, trying to remember the place where Louis had once dragged him for the final rites of a friend. There was no large advertisement, but in the smallest possible type it was listed at the old address on Spadina Avenue. An old man with the kind of accent Louis only imitated for the purpose of doing business downtown, answered the telephone.

"My grandfather's dead."

"Get a doctor," said the man. "With some people you never know."

"He's dead."

"Get a doctor first. Then we'll come and dress him for you. Don't worry."

At the funeral home they left the coffin open. In it, Louis Zackman was dressed in his best black suit, a yarmulke, and the blue tie he always hated. Harvey bent over the coffin, forcing himself. In the three nights since Louis's death, Harvey had slept only a few hours. He had learned to pace the narrow halls of his town house, carrying the candle he had bought to console himself, a white mourner's wax candle in a glass; and he had begun, in the midst of his sleeplessness, to discover himself kneeling inappropriately on the white shag carpet of his library, trying to pray.

"If there's a God," Louis Zackman used to say, "there's some things he should attend to."

But in these three nights Harvey did not know the feeling of God's eye on his soul. All he felt was one generation closer to the grave. "Soon it will be me," he thought. Again he was aware of his own skin, the imperfections he had at first ignored but now saw as signposts to his own death.

"It's natural to be afraid," Sarah Chernik told him. "To be afraid of your own fear is the worst."

"That sounds familiar."

"You can't afford to be clever now, Harvey."

This spoken in the darkness of Harvey's bedroom, exactly one mile from the Princess Margaret Hospital for Cancer. And when he bent over his grandfather's coffin, looking at the freshly pinked cheeks, Harvey suddenly saw Dorothy on the edge of his vision; she had interrupted her weeping to inspect him curiously, as if his own mixed anger and shame were equally painted on his face.

As the service started, old drunks at the back of the chapel chanted and muttered in company. These derelicts, unknown of course to the family, were a compulsory part of the funeral, and in accordance with the mortician's instructions Harvey had tried to pay for their good graces, handing out a whole pocketful of two-dollar bills.

He was so tired that even the harsh music of the prayers was soothing. He had been forced to study Hebrew, learned to read and write the characters so he could follow in the book, but he didn't actually understand more than a few words. So finally he found it most restful just to close his eyes and listen to the hired cantor, a hoarse-voiced man who poured out his messages to God in a quick river of half-articulated phrases countered by false trills and moans, drawn-out high notes far beyond his reach. With his hands in his pockets, shoulders hunched and bent, tears beginning to collect, Harvey rocked back and forth on his bench, trying to remember his grandfather.

And then the rabbi, sleek with a complacently round face and shiny black suit, began to deliver the penultimate tribute. "We who knew him," he began. But of course he hadn't. Harvey, with his father's help, had needed to supply the rabbi with the details of Louis Zackman's life so this elegy could be constructed, and as the rabbi spoke, the mutterings of the drunks grew louder and began to escalate into outright laughter. Looking back, Harvey could see them: indeterminately old men in shabby suits with paper-wrapped bottles in their hands, leaning against the back railing and sitting in the last row, gossiping and joking as if even the Last Judgment would only be another free movie. And in some strange way Harvey felt comforted by their presence, even while other members of the family were trying to shut them up, because the rented rabbi and cantor could never have known or cared about Louis Zackman, but these old drunks, in palmier days, might actually have shopped at Zackman's store, bought cheap furniture on credit and paid three times its worth in interest, and at least now they were getting something back from Louis Zackman, one last laugh.

The era after Bella died and the store became Zackman's Furniture was when Harvey entered high school. By the time Louis Zackman had returned to the pursuit of The Universal Miracle, Harvey had started to learn about science, which Louis always extolled, the wonderful perfect way in which the whole universe was made up of billiard balls, each set assembled in a tiny replica of the solar system, tricky billiard balls which could themselves break apart into an infinity of fragments and in doing so, according to Albert Einstein and others, possibly blow up the whole world.

During bomb drill, while kneeling under his desk with his hands crossed over the back of his neck to protect his medulla oblongata, Harvey would think about the marvels of science and especially Louis and the crazy filter he had attached to his new automobile.

In the midst of the depression, when he first worked on the project, Zackman had lacked test vehicles. Now, with the riches he had forcibly inherited from Bella's safe, he had purchased a long black Oldsmobile with silver trim.

"He was a wise and moderate man," said the rabbi. "A man who knew where his own universe ended and God's began." Nothing could have been further from the truth about Louis Zackman: his universe never ended, not for other people or for God. After blowing three engines out of the Oldsmobile, he began to connect his filters in series, trying two and three designs at once, so whereas at first it would take him two months to ruin a motor, eventually he could do it in a week.

After school, Harvey would have to clean and dust the furniture, wash windows, procure coffee for Louis Zackman and tea for his father; and there was no place in the store from which he couldn't see out front to where the black Oldsmobile stood. It was in fact, as he pointed out to his friends, nothing less than his mother's hearse, bought with her death money, and every time more cash from the store was poured into it, Harvey was further rankled. Until one day when Louis Zackman poked his long finger into Harvey's chest, Harvey poked back and began to scream.

"Science knows nothing of anger," Louis finally said.

"Oh, take your damn—" And that was all. His throat was raw, he didn't know what to say, he stomped out of the front door and up the side stairs to the apartment above the store; there he went into his own old room and helplessly knelt in the position of atomic attack.

* * *

At the graveyard, everyone waited around in the cold until the coffin finally arrived. With a great clanking of chains, tipping and threatening to spill open, it was lowered into the grave; and as it went down, and after it was resting, the drunken professional mourners rained stones upon it. Which thunked mutedly into the cheap composition board of the coffin, making only the occasionally satisfying clang at the hinges and trim.

Over this absurd and disturbing noise the rabbi began to read the final prayers, but as clods of earth and larger rocks succeeded the pebbles, the words got confused. Without knowing it, Harvey had started crying; he was holding onto Dorothy while her skinny arm dug through his wool coat, holding onto her and crying for the first time since his mother died. Then, cutting across and above his own voice, he heard a high quavering wail: it was his father. Stanley, standing on Dorothy's other side, had thrown his hat into the grave and was rocking back and forth, his high voice keening across the empty cemetery. Soon others joined in; the combined chorus grew so loud that the rabbi was silenced. Harvey looked at him, the treeless grounds, the apartment buildings that stood in the gray sky looking like particularly large monuments, and then he closed his eyes and began to cry again, letting himself be filled and carried by the sound, until finally the city disappeared, his self-consciousness disappeared, and he began to grow in his soul the image of the grandfather he had once known: Louis Zackman—wing-headed, stocky and muscular, The Universal Miracle printed into his genes.

When he opened his eyes, others were opening theirs, too, looking around, embarrassed.

"That was the way it used to be," Dorothy said. "At home; I remember now."

At his own home, Sarah Chernik was waiting for him and the kitchen was filled with the steam of cooking. Wearing a turban around her head, olive skin perspiring in the heat, cheeks flushed as his own had been, she turned to him as he walked in the door.

"What are you doing here?"

"I felt like cooking. How was the funeral?"

"Terrible."

"You look nice."

He was wearing a black striped suit he had bought only a month before, and with it a white silk shirt. But only now, as he poured himself a drink, did he realize that for Louis Zackman's funeral he had dressed himself up in his best clothes, everything from his Spanish patent leather boots to the Cardin tie for which he had paid twenty-five dollars.

"That was the way it used to be," Dorothy had said, and with a weird but contented smile on her face had sat proudly between Stanley and Harvey as they drove back to the suburban split-level house Louis Zackman had bought with the profits of Bella's early demise. The whole family came too; a funeral not followed by drinks and food could not be imagined, and while the distant uncles and cousins drank their straight scotch and brandy and ate stale cookies and buns provided by the funeral home, Harvey sat on the corner sofa with his father.

"With a Zackman, all things end at the stomach," Louis used to say. In fact, even his cancer had ended there, after progressing downward from his chest, the exploded particles and mutant cells following inside him the voyage his planetary crust had taken years before. And as Harvey stood in his kitchen, watching this woman trying to console him with food, he couldn't force out of his mind the image of Stanley, now endowed with a new aggressive confidence, voraciously attacking the food and spreading crumbs about himself like manna.

Stanley, with Louis's death, had prospered. Stanley, who after the sale of the store came back into his parents' house, a room with its own bathroom in the basement, now seemed to have doubled in size. When he stood up to greet newcomers at the door, his back straightened, his voice lowered. After the drive home, he had uncharacteristically leapt out of the car and held the door open for Dorothy. Now it could almost be believed he would move upstairs.

All through Sarah Chernik's dinner, Harvey worked at his scotch. Afterward they danced; her hand pressed warmly into his back, he let himself be led through the house, stumbling, laughing, secretly crying, he moved from room to room with her, trying to feel the warmth coming into his own deadened body, trying to let her exorcise the ghost.

But it was only late that night, with Sarah gone home and the house dark and silent, that Harvey finally began to get drunk.

With each sip, he felt new radioactive particles invent themselves and explode beneath his skin. "Science can do anything," his grandfather had said. Smiling beneficently at Harvey, he drove him every day from the downtown store to the bright suburban bungalow, the works of the black Oldsmobile purring with its magical filters. And even on the very last day of his scientific career, when a piston flew up and through the shining black hood, pierced the gleaming clean wraparound windshield, and came sharply to rest in the seat between Louis Zackman and his skeptical wife, Dorothy, even on that day Zackman's grandson was put to bed with a book about the wonderful world of the microscope.

Holding his scotch in one hand and his wax-filled mourner's glass in the other, Harvey stumbled up and down the narrow stairs of his town house, going from one shag-carpeted room to the next, until he finally ended up in the library. There he went down on his knees, but though he tried to remember the words of the funeral prayers they escaped him; all he seemed to know was the blessing for bread. As he repeated that over and over to himself, the sound of the words melted into the earth and rocks homing into the coffin; and the sight of his own praying dissolved into old men's faces, drunk and delighted to be paid in two-dollar bills to stand and kibbitz during a funeral, old men's faces laughing at these crazy Jews so lost from themselves they needed professionals to stone a cheap coffin down to the grave.

THE SECRET

She is like the shadow of a cloud upon the water.
  She is like the sound of wind through absent trees.
  In the sun her hair is golden.
  At night she is dark. She moves with the sea and is invisible.
Her voice is conducted by rumors and bones.

* * *

To get to Sydney's house, you go down to the harbor where the
fish boats tie up, and cross the bridge to the western side of the
slough. Sydney's house is old and made out of green-painted
cedar; it is sheltered, almost hidden, by two old yew trees whose
branches poke through the small and unused porch of the house,
poke through the outhouse roof and now begin to threaten the
windows of the second floor. Sydney says that he is fifty-one years
old. He lies on his couch and sometimes he wheezes. His false
teeth are on the mantelpiece, upper and lower, unconnected by
hinges or springs, the individual plates looking unrelated, the
lower one hooked and elongated as if it were meant for the jaw of
a fish, more gum than teeth even though they are unused. Last
week Sydney ate eggs. "Can't get enough eggs," Sydney said. Said
this twice an hour, lying sunk into his back on the old compliant
couch, slapped his leg and laughed. Sydney lies on his back and
looks out his window to the tiny harbor. He is thinking about the
secret or at least he is pretending. "They say if you eat too many

eggs it swells up the blood," Sydney says. Even without his teeth he speaks clearly, like a bloated shark. Sydney has worn his teeth only a few times, mostly for the dentist. "They say if you eat too many eggs it swells up the blood," Sydney repeats. He winks with both eyes at once and laughs. His eyes are narrow and his face fat. His whole body is fat. Today Sydney is thinking about washing the ceiling. Last night he was drunk. Tomorrow Sydney will walk vacantly about the streets, circling blocks carefully like a new arrival, navigating all the events that he remembers, searching through the village until he comes to a store that will sell him some soap to use in his old metal bucket, the same bucket his mother used for washing walls and floors. Every afternoon Sydney lies on the couch. The couch is covered with a green-fringed spread that was guaranteed never to wear out. When his mother bought it from the catalogue.

* * *

The secret moves about the world and is seen in different places.

The secret is expected.

The secret could fly through the sky like a square-winged eagle, drop on her prey like an avenging angel, appear in church at Easter if she wanted.

* * *

Sydney knows the times of all the tides. He knows there is a comet coming. It will shine in the sky day and night. Never stopping. "Maybe the secret will come with the comet," Harry Sampson says.

"The secret won't come until leap year," Peter Coulter says.

Harry Sampson and Peter Coulter own fish boats. In the evening Sydney goes down to the wharves, watches the men unwind and clean their nets. Their fingers are tough and brown.

This week Sydney is eating eggs again.

This week Sydney tells what Peter Coulter said. "Maybe he spoke out of turn," Sydney says.

Sydney is lying on his couch in the house his parents left him when they died. He has Indian friends. They bring whiskey and fish for him. Sometimes they stay in his house and vomit in the sink. Sometimes the young white people stay in his house too. They help Sydney eat and drink. Sometimes they bring up and sometimes they clean up. That is the way it is at Sydney's house, unchanging except for the objects and heirlooms, all worthless, which gradually disappear as the visitors stream through. No one has yet stolen the violin. It is in the dining room, on the buffet, still there but missing its strings, its pegs and its bridge, as if it is being sneaked out gradually by an inexperienced thief.

"Do you play the violin?"

"Sure," Sydney says. "I played the violin but my hands got too fat." He laughs and laughs. Everybody talks about the way Sydney laughs, the way you have to laugh with him because you can't help it. He laughs and slaps the couch. "That's a good one, eh?" He laughs. "A good one on me."

"You could play the violin for the secret when she comes."

Sydney doesn't reply. He stares out the window across the slough where the boats are tied up. "I couldn't play the violin for anyone," Sydney says. "My hands are too fat." He laughs. He looks out the window. His eyes are small and lost in the places where his cheeks puff up. Last winter he got a job sweeping the streets of Masset. For three dollars an hour he walked up and down with a wire-brush broom, pushing the water from the center of the road to the ditches. Sometimes it rains too hard for working outside. The rain carries away the garbage. Even in the summer there is a lot of rain and not much garbage. In the winter there is more rain. The town is small, the kind of town that someone always has schemes for. Last year it was a kelp factory. In the hotel there is a clear plastic bag containing the first kelp processed by the factory. It looks like parsley or marijuana or anything green. This year they are talking about reopening the factory, converting it into a potato-chip plant. Soon there will be shiny silver bags for Sydney's wire broom. The company is conducting a survey.

* * *

Soon the tide will be in.
  The secret moves like the tide.
  In the spring she grows green with the bushes.
  In the sun her hair is golden.
  Sydney's wedding ring is golden, too.

* * *

At night Sydney's golden wedding ring is mellow in the light of the kerosene lamps. "Peter Coulter told me that this ring would turn my finger green," Sydney says. His laughs are long dolls'-chains of giggles. Sometimes he wakes up in the middle of the night and laughs the same way. "Don't look green to me," Sydney says. He spends a week inspecting his finger. "Don't look green to me," Sydney says. He laughs and shifts deeper into the cushions. He is thinking of washing the ceiling. "Got to wash the ceiling before the secret comes," Sydney says. He has heard the secret is in Panama. Or was it Vancouver? They say she'll be in Burnaby before the next full moon. They say she's selling jewelry in Mexico, string pearl necklaces, yellow agates as big as oranges, golden wedding rings.

  This week Sydney is eating eggs. This week the moon is a crescent. This week the tides are high, eroding the banks of the slough, gouging out more sand, toppling two cedars that had survived the past few years, their roots exposed, waiting for this high water. The trees will still live. They will stick out from the bank, hanging over the beach, and stay green until there are more storms, erosions. Sydney lies on the couch with his hands clasped about his stomach. Today Sydney has decided not to eat eggs. Today Sydney has decided that eggs will bloat him further, extend him beyond the capacities of the couch and send him rolling onto the hooked-rug his mother's mother made.

* * *

The secret passes like a shadow across the water.
  The secret sighs like the sound of wind through absent trees.

The secret eats antelopes, burps up great quantities of garlic and Portuguese red wine.

The secret whispers. She tells me that my bones are hollow. Her bones are hollow. Rattles and drums. The secret fishes for her own spirit.

* * *

Sometimes Sydney goes to bed but cannot sleep. Every night at twenty to ten he takes off his clothes and puts on his blue flannel pajamas. He climbs into bed and blows out the kerosene lamp. From the attic I hear the bed sigh with his weight. Sydney is so fat it is possible he outweighs his parents. Sydney is so old it is possible the bed is simply weary of this succession of flesh. Maybe it is the nature of the bed to creak. I go through these possibilities. Sydney is a hypnotist. People around him begin to talk like Sydney. I am upstairs and there is another boarder on the first floor, in the bedroom that was Sydney's when his parents were alive. "Good morning," we say to each other. We giggle and slap our thighs. We argue about the day of the week. We take turns brushing Sydney's false teeth. "The secret is like a bowl of corn flakes," I say. The other boarder is a woman. She is attractive, but in this house I am blind to her. When I see her on the street I want to take her home with me, but when I take her home with me I don't know what to say. We talk about rumors and keep Sydney's house clean.

"Who are you?" Sydney says when I come into the room. It's important to sit down when he talks. I sit down.

"It's okay, Sydney," I say. "It's just me."

"It's just me," Sydney says. "It's just me and today's today and that's all I know." He slaps his knee and laughs. Tomorrow he will tell everyone I said I was just me. "It's just me," Sydney will say and he will slap his knee. Now that he doesn't like eggs he eats porridge three times a day. Sydney's bed reconciles itself to one more night.

Some nights Sydney wakes up in the middle of the night and laughs. Some nights Sydney can't sleep. The bed reconciles itself but Sydney stays awake. Then he gets up and puts on a huge shapeless gray coat and explores the town streets. Sometimes he walks across the slough, east to the adjacent village, where the Indians live. Sometimes he goes down to the hotel to sit in the lounge. People know him and offer to buy him drinks. He orders exotic concoctions. It is somehow disconcerting to come across Sydney upright. He sits in the red upholstered chair wearing his gray coat. All its stains and tears and patches add up to so many different stories that they have canceled each other out. His skin is pale white, protected from the sun by the rain and by his afternoons on the couch. On his couch he has wasted enough time to read ten encyclopedias; to succeed or fail at three careers; to be in the Army and get honorably retired with a pension; to be on the sea for decades and now be an old man good for three more decades of outrageous lies and tales; to marry twice and have ten grandchildren; to break the world record for counting to the highest number ever arrived at, one by one, by any North American male born in this century.

"Well, today's today and that's all I know," Sydney says.

"For sure," I agree. I have come down from my room. The woman boarder is up, too. She has bought the missing parts for the violin. Now that Sydney is home from the lounge we have a surprise for him. We wait until he is settled into his couch. He has had a lot to drink but isn't going to vomit tonight. He is wearing his gray coat and his feet are tucked into their customary cushion. He looked at himself in the mirror in the men's washroom. He tells us about it. He tells us that he saw his face and it looked back at him and it said, "Sydney, why are you looking at me?" The woman boarder has tuned the violin. The only song she knows how to play is "God Save the Queen." She says that if she practices maybe she could remember something better but there isn't any time. Sydney is lying on the couch and we are about to give him the surprise, but now he stands up and removes his coat. Then he picks up the lantern and stumbles over to the mantelpiece. The mantelpiece isn't attached to anything, it is just something that must have been salvaged from a house now defunct. It sits on top of some bookshelves. When his false teeth are in, Sydney gets back into the couch.

"Sometimes a man needs his teeth," Sydney says.

"For sure," the woman boarder says. Every day for a week we have been responding to Sydney with the same phrase, waiting for him to try it. So far he doesn't seem to have noticed.

"He wouldn't say anything even if he did" was my opinion.

"Sydney always speaks his mind," the woman boarder said. Maybe she was right. I never spoke my mind in Sydney's house. I could never locate it there. It didn't seem to matter.

"Did you ever see my chest?" Sydney asked.

"You're a married man," the woman boarder said.

"I don't know," Sydney said. "Sometimes I think she's never going to come. She was supposed to come the last full moon and she didn't come. Now she's supposed to come the next full moon. I don't know."

"You're just depressed because you're drunk," the woman boarder said.

"I'm not drunk," Sydney said. He reached out for the back of the sofa, pulled at it until he was sitting up. His face was swollen around his unaccustomed teeth. "I could play the violin," Sydney said. He laughed and slapped his knee. With his teeth in he had to laugh cautiously, be careful not to swallow them. I got the violin for him from its place in the dining room. I handed it to him. Sydney tucked it under his chin. He grabbed the bow wholly, like a child closing his fist around a candy cane. He pushed the bow back and forth across the strings. It didn't sound like anything but it didn't sound like nothing. It sounded exactly as it should have, notes scratched out one after the other, in no order that could be understood, not pretending to be anything except noise. Someone else might have have said it sounded like a rusty key in a lock.

* * *

Sydney is fifty-one years old.

The secret moves like the shadow passing across a new moon.

The secret talks like a man playing the violin.

It is fall and in the evening Sydney's friends go out into the slash, carrying rifles beneath their arms and listening for the sounds of frightened deer.

* * *

When Sydney is finished playing the violin he hands the bow and the instrument to the woman boarder. He takes his teeth out and throws them behind the couch. The woman boarder stands awkwardly in front of the couch with the violin. Sydney looks normal again, drunk, his mouth small and sunken. "Who are you?" Sydney says to her while she holds the violin. Everything is normal. She begins to play "God Save the Queen." While she plays she faces out the window. When she is finished she hands the violin to me and I take it to its place, in the dining room. I didn't want to look at Sydney while she was playing, but now I see him sitting on the couch. He has taken off his shirt and is showing his chest. It is covered with charts of the tides, figures and calculations. They don't seem to be anything. In some places the tattoos look fresh, tiny scabs still clinging to the skin. At night when Sydney can't sleep he goes for walks in his shapeless coat. During the day he dozes on the couch. When Sydney is finished explaining his chest he puts on his shirt. "That's a good one, eh?" Sydney says. He doesn't laugh. The woman boarder and I help him on with his shirt. He stands up and we are both supporting him, one at each arm. We help him into his bedroom and ease him down onto the bed. The springs squeak and protest. The woman boarder sits down beside him and she is holding his hand. She is holding the hand with the ring. In the light the ring is golden, and while she is holding his hand she twists the ring on his finger, absently, as if his hand were part of her own body. "Sometimes I think the secret's never going to come," Sydney says.

"That's all right," the woman boarder says.

"For sure," the woman boarder says.

"For sure," Sydney says. He burps. The woman boarder stays sitting on the bed and I go upstairs. From my room I can hear the night sounds of Sydney shifting in his bed. The tree scratches against the window. In my own bed the covers enclose me, are heavy across my back and neck like a cowl. I have no ring and no false teeth. In the morning I will go downstairs and see if Sydney has been sick.

HEYFITZ

An anonymous man, let us call him Franz, discovers one day that he has been fatally wounded. He decides to approach his end in a languorous way, and dresses himself in dark trousers, blue silk shirt, a mustache he has found by the washstand.

In this fatal moment, twilight is his time. He lies in the arms of a beautiful anonymous woman and he prepares to confess. "God," he says, "have I ever asked you any favors before?"

He sinks deep into the arms of his beloved. One more time? Why not. Records change, the sun sinks lower into the hills, all else remains posted.

Afterward Franz washes himself carefully, but finds his wound has still not gone away. He prepares to look in the mirror, to see in his aging and tragic face the most hopeless of all creatures. Instead he discovers that it is two weeks since he has shaved. At that moment, Franz realizes he need fear no wound, no matter how fatal, for he has never existed.

* * *

Franz woke up hearing voices. Even his name had a familiar ring.

"Franz?" called his wife.

"Yes?"

"Do you want to speak on the telephone?"

It was while putting the receiver to his ear that Franz looked down and saw that his wound remained, unchanged.

"Franz," said a stranger's voice. "How are you enjoying your vacation?" From the kitchen, Franz could hear the sounds of eggs breaking against the iron skillet. It reminded him of the sea.

"Very well," Franz said. "Very well."

"We hope you will soon return," said the voice. Franz put his hand over the mouthpiece and scratched at his beard. The Spanish sun slanted in the window and blinded him. Or was it Spain? It might have been Italy.

"Franz," said the voice. "I'm talking to you."

"Yes." It was too late for disguises. "You'll have to excuse me," Franz said, and placed the receiver back on the hook. Then he walked into the kitchen and sat down in front of his breakfast. Dolores his wife was named, dolorous. He sometimes liked to make jokes about her name: his favorite was that he had met her at a funeral, where she was employed as a professional mourner.

"Franz," she said.

"Yes?"

"Are you feeling better?"

"Was I sick?"

"Of course not," his wife said. "Who ever told you you were sick?" She looked at him. He looked at her. They often liked to try to fool each other this way. It was also one of their games. Another: to stand on the balcony, wrapped in a towel, disguised as a politician speaking to the masses. Yet another: to cook each other little mystery dinners dressed in scalloped potatoes and Chinese lettuce. They looked at each other. Franz thought he knew what was going on in his wife's mind. He thought she was looking at him and thinking: Franz, this is good-by. I'm so sorry you're sick. I'll live forever, whereas for you, I'm afraid, this is good-by. He could imagine her at his funeral. She was, after all, a professional.

"Franz?" she said.

"Yes."

"Who are you? Really?"

"Who are you?" he returned.

"I'll tell you later," said Dolores. Was she bluffing?

They looked at each other. Franz scratched his nose, expecting to find his false mustache. But it had fallen off during the night and now Franz was left alone.

* * *

When Franz returned to the city, two months had passed. His wound had grown into an illness, and one afternoon he found himself in the office of a famous doctor.

"How do you feel?" asked the doctor.

"Sick."

Franz was sitting on the consulting table, his long white shirt hanging modestly to his knees. The doctor stood in front of him, looking at him absently, as if he were an X-ray photograph.

"What are your symptoms?"

"They're hard to describe," Franz said. "I feel pains in different places. Sometimes I wake up and am sore all over. Other times I don't wake up at all; I sleep right through."

"Through what?" asked the doctor. He had a voice that cannot be described.

"I don't know," Franz said. "That's just it. I feel I'm missing something." He looked hopelessly at the doctor. A new suspicion was entering his mind. "Are you working for my wife?"

"No," said the doctor sharply, in his indescribable voice.

"I was just testing you," Franz said. He laughed. It was the first time he had laughed in two months, for on the morning of the telephone conversation his wife had left him without even doing the dishes.

"Do I pass the test?" asked the doctor.

"Of course," Franz said. "If you weren't going to pass, I wouldn't have invented you."

The eminent doctor stroked his chin. He began tapping at Franz's knees with a small rubber hammer. He took his temperature, his blood pressure, made him piss into a bottle.

"Do you know what's wrong with you?" the doctor finally asked.

"No," said Franz. Although he had his own ideas. The doctor put on his glasses and prepared to give his diagnosis. The door opened. In came a nurse. Before either of them could protest, she began to disrobe in an unobtrusive way. At the last moment Franz realized that this was his own wife. The doctor had fooled him after all.

"What are you doing here?"

"Oh, it's you," she said, pretending to be surprised.

* * *

They used to have different games. For example: the first time he stayed away for a week, he came home to find Dolores drunk, in the bathtub with a stranger. She had forgotten to run the water. The stranger was a new cat. "Hello," she said when she opened her eyes; and acted as if he had never left. Nothing he said could make her admit something unusual had happened.

Another example: one day she was telling him about her former lovers—at his insistence. He was growing increasingly uncomfortable and jealous. To console himself he put on his false mustache and began to smoke a cigar. "I have to tell you this," she whispered. "Joseph Stalin used to take baths in pickle juice in order to preserve himself." At this unfortunate moment one of Franz's mistresses arrived in the dumbwaiter, wearing a compromising costume.

A final example: the cat was always changing. One week it was tabby, the next Persian, the next Siamese, et cetera. Neither of them would admit to changing the cat, yet they never had the same cat twice. It always answered to the name of Heyfitz.

"Heyfitz," Franz would say.

The cat would look at him.

"Heyfitz, today I'm going to teach you how to juggle." Franz believed that it would be unusual to have a juggling cat. He had even found out the true secret of successful juggling: it is to keep the eye on the top ball. Sometimes he would succeed in teaching Heyfitz the first elementary maneuvers. But then the week would end, and Heyfitz would be changed.

It should be said that Franz was completely taken in by this particular game. He was so surprised by it each week that he never once said good-by, and there finally came a time when he believed Dolores could change cats in the dark.

* * *

"I'll tell you what you have," the doctor said. They were alone again and it was twilight. All signs of the struggle had been erased by the setting sun and Franz felt an obscure victorious warmth creeping through his belly. Of course he had dressed again. He and the doctor were sitting in the famous man's library, looking over a few medical texts from the Dark Ages.

"The trouble with you," said the doctor, "is that you invented yourself. As is common in such delusions, you began to believe you invented others, too. Your wife, for example."

"Oh, no," Franz said. "I wouldn't have invented her."

"So you say," said the doctor.

To pass the time, they began to play a game of chess. As Franz was elongating the Sicilian Defense—or perhaps it was only a variation of the Italian Opening—he saw that a cat had entered the room. "Heyfitz," he said. The cat jumped into his lap. The doctor looked at him suspiciously.

"You see?" the doctor said. "You invented that cat."

"No, I didn't. I never saw it before."

Heyfitz stretched slowly, then went over to the buffet and began to juggle three small oranges.

"That's amazing," the doctor admitted. He became extremely demoralized. His play deteriorated, slid downhill; moves followed each other like badly rolled cigarettes. Soon Franz had the eminent doctor trapped in a deep cul-de-sac from which there was no escape.

"I'm afraid it's all over for you," said Franz, surveying the board.

"Not for me," the doctor said. "I have to tell you one more thing." He looked at Franz darkly. "If you're not inventing me, I must be inventing you. Ha ha." He reached down and had a brilliant stroke. "Checkmate," he said indescribably.

* * *

The next morning, Franz's illness was worse: he discovered that he was turning into himself. He stared at his face in the mirror:

his eyes, blankly burning, stared back, waiting to be released. It was almost three months since he had shaved. He scratched his beard and brushed his teeth.

"Heyfitz," Franz called.

The cat came into the bathroom. This week it was Persian, with long white fur.

"Heyfitz," Franz said. "Who do I remind you of?" Heyfitz looked at him carefully, shrugged his white shoulders and walked out.

"All right," Franz said. "I know what you mean." He dressed himself in a dark suit, a white shirt, and a tie. He combed back his thinning hair and put on his sunglasses. Before going outside he made himself a cup of coffee and looked out the window of his apartment. Rivers of traffic passed each other by. Dozens of people stood out on the street, oblivious to everything except the feel of the morning sun on their faces. Franz opened the window. The air rushed in: a mixture of exhaust fumes, restaurant smells, late-summer flowers, flesh wet and powdered for the day.

"All right," Franz said again. "I know what you mean." He turned back to the room. While he was looking out the window Heyfitz had been changed. He was now a lazy black cat with thick glossy fur.

"Heyfitz," Franz said.

The cat blinked.

"You could have fooled me," Franz said. He felt that the situation was deteriorating. "I hope you'll excuse me," he said to Heyfitz. "But I don't have time to teach you how to juggle. Keep your eye on the top ball." On the way out the door, he looked in the mirror once more: eyes, lips, nose—even the lines on his forehead—everything was exactly in place, exactly as it should be, exactly *him*.

Franz closed the door behind him and walked down the stairs and out onto the street. His apartment was above a small grocery store. Placed outside it were wooden crates of fruits and vegetables, their skins glistening green, red, yellow, lighting up the shadows like wet jewels. The owner of the store was standing beside his produce, spraying it against the day's heat. He nodded at

Franz without speaking. Franz nodded back, also without speaking. It was their only game.

With his hands in his pockets, Franz began to walk down the street. Cars, store windows, people, telephone poles, dogs—all swept by in a confused flood. When he got hot, Franz bought an ice cream cone and stood in the shade of a striped awning. With his dark suit, his undone tie, his short thinning hair, Franz looked like a professional mourner. "Dolores," Franz said. She had often dressed up as him, putting on one of his suits and hiding in a cupboard to surprise him. Now, finally, when it was too late, he was returning the favor. "Dolores," Franz said again. A warm victorious feeling crept into his stomach. Somehow he had swallowed her without meaning to.

It was high noon in the city. The sun shone desperately, trying to reach through the pavement, the underground pipes and sewers, the subways that had never been completed—trying to reach through the smoke, and the dirt, and the toys of the city, to the earth. It didn't succeed. Franz finished his cone and wiped his mouth against his coat. It was a poor day to be wearing a suit, but the occasion was special.

"Heyfitz," Franz said. He looked around. He had finally realized that they were using Heyfitz to follow him.

* * *

Franz resumed his walk. In a few minutes he had reached his objective, the university: it was a tall gray building that stretched sixty stories up into the air. The lobby was veneered with black spotted marble and elevator doors. Each of the sixty floors of the university represented an entire realm of man's existence; and of course they were completely separate from each other. But Franz didn't go to any of them. Instead he descended the stairs into the basement and made his way through the irregular corridors.

Presently he encountered a small stooped man who was pushing a broom along the granite floor. Over his shoulder he carried a small sack filled with a day's supply of Dustbane.

"How are you doing?" Franz asked.

"I can't complain," said the old man. He leaned the broom against the wall and examined his son. "What's wrong with you?"

"I don't know," Franz began. Then he saw what the old man was staring at. "I decided to grow a beard."

The old man shook his head and muttered, as if he had heard this a thousand times before. He took out a stub of a cigarette and lit it.

"I thought you were going to stop smoking," Franz said.

"How is your wife?" the old man asked in a sly voice.

"Well," Franz began.

"Tell me later." The old man took Franz by the elbow and gently led him to a deserted corner of the corridor, where they found some old wooden chairs and a kettle. The old man chopped up one of the chairs and started a fire while Franz filled the kettle from a nearby fountain.

When their tea was boiled, the old man smiled at Franz and signaled him to begin again. They looked alike, these two men: father and son. One was older, of course. And the other had a beard.

"It was at the doctor's," Franz said. "There was an accident." He looked into the eyes of his father. They were the color of burnished eggplant. "There was a game we used to play," said Franz. "One of us would stand at the open window and say to the other—Mother, push me." Telling his father this reminded Franz of other games they used to play together, in the bathtub. "She's still around," Franz said helplessly. "She's still changing the cat." His father blinked sympathetically at him.

"I'm sick," Franz admitted. "I don't feel right these days. Things seem to be going out of control. Do you ever get that feeling?" His hands began to tremble and he spilled his cup of tea. "God-damn smoke," Franz said. He kicked the fire apart. "Why don't they ventilate this place properly?" He looked at his father. His father looked back, sadly. It was years since they had seen each other. If they had had any games, they had forgotten them. "Heyfitz," Franz called. "HEYFITZ!" He looked around desperately. Nothing. He handed his empty cup back to his father. "I'm sorry," he said. "I have to go. Good-by." He looked at his father, snapped his fingers nervously, then ran down the corridor until he found his way to the stairs.

* * *

Outside, Franz felt worse than ever. It was hot. The afternoon was filled with vapors and smoke. He took off his jacket and laid it on a bench. Then he started home, walking and running, his breath so short that by the time he got to the grocery store his lungs were burning and his ribs felt as if they were tearing apart.

The owner was still wearing his white smock, still standing in front of his fruits and vegetables, keeping them freshly wet. He nodded at Franz. Franz nodded at him.

"What happened to your eggplants?" Franz said. This was a new ploy. He had never spoken to the man before.

The grocer laughed. "Eggplants? I never had any."

"All right," Franz said aggressively. "I was only asking." He paused. Now that they were talking, anything could happen.

"Have you seen my wife?" asked Franz.

"Is she missing? What happened to her?"

"Nothing," Franz said. Their first silence had been broken. Their second silence now began. It was empty. Franz nodded. The grocer nodded back. "See you later," Franz said.

The grocer refused to reply.

Franz went up the stairs and into the apartment. As soon as he was inside, he locked the door and went into the bathroom to inspect himself in the mirror. His eyes glowed, his beard was growing full, his hair had receded farther, leaving intimations of a skull. Inside his chest he could feel his heart beating, trapped by his ribs. He looked at himself. Pounding heart, burning eyes: somehow they had gone out of control. A new possibility entered his brain. "What if I exist?" Franz asked himself. "What if I am?" He remembered the first game he had ever played with his wife. They had taken off all their clothes and pretended they were strangers. He put his hand to his chest. He could feel his heart struggling like a dying animal.

"Heyfitz," he called. "Heyfitz."

No one appeared.

Franz went into the living room. "Heyfitz," he called. A noise made him turn around. In the corner was standing the eminent doctor, wrapped in a glossy black fur coat and juggling three oranges. He looked at Franz sadly. On the window sill was crouched the shadow of Dolores, not quite hidden by the setting sun.

"Heyfitz," called Franz. The doctor was wearing a black velvet hat and his eyes shone out like wet yellow jewels.

"All right," Franz said. "I know what you mean."

DEATH OF
A FRIEND

I heard the news shortly after it happened. It was near the end of August, during one of those late-summer heat waves that sometimes hold Toronto to ransom, a night I hadn't slept at all but only lain on top of the sheet, trying to convince myself that the fan was doing something. Even though I was awake, I hesitated to answer the telephone when it rang. When I did, Marion's voice cut through the night with its usual abruptness.

"Gavin's killed himself," she said.

"What?"

"Gavin's dead."

At my age, which is thirty-eight—going on fifty, it sometimes seems—I have learned to be prepared for the death of a friend. But not Gavin, who was more than a friend, who was at the least indestructible. I tried to say something. The noise of the fan's motor filled the room: a giant insect seeking somewhere to land.

"Are you all right?" Marion has a harsh voice that cannot give anything away.

"Sure," I said. "I'm all right." I had pushed myself up and was lighting a cigarette. "Where are you?"

"I'm at the hospital." The fan and her voice were melting together, shivering and buzzing in my skull, her words blurred into tiny motors. "I'm just standing at a pay phone in the emergency room."

"Do you want me to come down there? Or can you come here?"

"I'll take a taxi. There's nothing left to do."

By the time I was dressed and had coffee on the stove, Marion was at the door. I live in an apartment in one of those increasingly rare Toronto houses—a rambling brick house that sits on a lot big enough for a high-rise. When I moved here, twelve years ago, other houses like this surrounded it. Now when I look out the window past the two oaks that survive in the front yard, I see metal balconies and concrete. But in the old days, when Gavin and Marion and I were close, and our lives mixed in so tightly we hardly knew ourselves as separate people, I could sometimes sit here in my living room, looking out at other windows as shaded and baroque as my own, and be completely held by the magic of this place.

I had unlatched the door, and Marion, as she used to, came in without knocking. I heard the sharp sounds of her shoes against the hardwood floor and then, suddenly—as if it were ten years ago—she was standing facing me in the kitchen, arms hanging helplessly at her sides.

"God-damned idiot," she said. "What did he have to do that for?" Anyone else who looked like Marion would have been beautiful; she had thick black hair, long and parted in the middle, small snubbed features, wide-set brown eyes and sensuous lips—all frozen into a determined mask by her amazing and inflexible will. In pictures she looked sensational; in person, as Gavin once said fondly, she looked like a dentist.

"Coffee or a drink?"

"A drink," she said. "I'm already drowning in machine coffee." Automatically she reached for the cupboard above the refrigerator where I kept the whiskey—close to the ice—and as if it weren't several years since she had even been in this apartment, she helped herself to what she needed. And, without asking, she made me a drink too—the way I used to like it—two shot glasses of scotch and two pieces of ice. "Can't trust city water," Gavin would say. He was a purist, and in his most religious moments he even omitted the ice.

We went and sat in the living room, Marion and I, the survivors. We sat side by side on the couch; and if ten years ago we had also been in this place—I insulting her and she yowling at me like an outraged cat—that only drew us closer now.

"Do you want to tell me?"

"I don't know." She found herself a cigarette and lit it carefully, moving her hands and fingers slowly—trying not to shake.

"It's been bad," I suggested. "I heard it had been bad with him lately."

"You know how he was," Marion said.

* * *

When I first met Gavin Donnally he was sitting behind his office desk—as old then as I am now. He was one of those men who attract rumors, and so I already knew about his legendary bottle a day, and about the novel he was supposed to have been working on for more than a decade: a brilliant huge novel that seemed never to get finished. In his hand he held a sheaf of papers, my own manuscript. It had taken me almost a year to write, though it was only a section of a projected novel; and I had no doubt that in Gavin's verdict rested my entire future. Although he wasn't yet forty, he looked much older. His faced was lined and aristocratic, his gray hair combed back from a widow's peak, and his eyes redrimmed and shadowed. Somehow, this mask of fatigue and dissipation only made him seem more romantic to me, a hero of success and failure.

In comparison, and sitting in his office I couldn't help making the judgment, I felt fat and callow. He must, I thought, see hundreds of hopeful young writers like myself every year, petitioning him with their crazy stories. My own, I now realized to my total embarrassment, must be even worse than most. At the time, Gavin had reached the final position of his career and was the senior editor of a large publishing house. The manuscript I had shown him was a long story, one of three I intended to make up a book that would depict—how can I put it?—my youth in a small town. In addition to having written the first, I was already well into the second, a sentimental rendition of my coming of age. And the third, the triumphant journey from the town to the city, lay glistening hopefully in my mind, needing only the slightest encouragement to be set down in all its splendor. Sitting across from Gavin Donnally, waiting for him to deliver his judgment, I already knew what it was.

"You'll have to excuse me."

"What?" Gavin always liked to say, "What?" in an aggressive way. He later explained that it gave him the edge in conversation —though I must admit I eventually decided he had drunk himself deaf.

"I shouldn't have wasted your time with the story."

"Oh, that." With a delicate gesture, he set down the offending manuscript and then flicked his fingers nervously, as if to clean them.

"It's not very good."

"Take off your coat," he said. Then he plugged in a kettle, preparing to make coffee. I measured out the implications of this: the necessary minutes to be consumed.

"I read your story," he said. "It's got something. A way with words. A feel for childhood. Something very touching.

When the water had boiled, we would discuss the contract.

"I understand it's part of a novel," he said. He was referring to my letter, in which I had explained the entire plan. As he spoke, I was reminding myself to buy another thousand sheets of yellow paper to start the final third.

"It's almost done," I said. "Maybe I should have waited to show you."

"No," Gavin said. He had a very considered and precise way of speaking, each word a neat little knife cutting through the messy world. "I'm glad you showed me now." He sighed unhappily.

"You can write," he said. "You do have a talent." He sighed again. My heart was exploding—this was it: cynical editor takes young novelist under wing. I would have to get a new suit. And a haircut. Maybe even contact lenses.

"You know," he said. His voice dropped. Later on I knew this meant he was moving in for the kill. "God knows you have talent.

And a real sentimental feeling for things. And yet. Somehow. It just doesn't make it. There it is."

He leaned across the desk to see how I was taking it. I remember how uncomfortable my mouth felt, frozen in mid-smile. I had hardly heard him—in fact I had been thinking about the size of my advance and only now was absorbing what he'd said.

"Well?" he asked, still aggressive.

"Well," I said. "There it is. But you think there's hope?"

"Oh, yes. There's always hope. You never know what someone might do. Especially someone as young as you. How old did you say you were?"

"Twenty-six."

"Oh. I thought you were younger."

"I see," I mumbled. But I didn't. Gavin smiled graciously at me —as if in fact he had just informed me that his firm would publish this and all my future works—sight unseen. Then he stood up and made us cups of instant coffee.

"I like your dialogue," he said. "Have you ever considered writing for television?"

"I never watch it."

"Maybe you should." And that was how we started, Gavin and I. When my first script was sold, I telephoned the news to him.

"Congratulations," he said. "Let me take you out to dinner."

* * *

In those days, Toronto was everything to me: the huge and anonymous arena where I would find myself, remake myself, succeed or fail according to the terms of my most obscure and central dreams. Now, of course, it's different. The invisible inner gleam has worn off, and Toronto is only the place where I live—a big paunchy complex city where I have somehow put down roots and am satisfied to play out my existence. Even if they tear down this house I suppose I will stay, living in another apartment, rewriting other people's television scripts, teaching my drama course at the university. In a way I have become like Gavin Donnally; older, thinner, more cynical—readier to fuel the ambitions of others than try my own again.

But then, with my first sale, the dream was at its brightest, and I could believe the future was in my blood. When I went to the restaurant, Gavin was there already, red roses at the table, and sitting with Marion, young then too—and if not beautiful, at least striking.

She was wearing a deep-cut black dress, looking expensive and sophisticated. Her face was composed, breaking apart only when Gavin said something that was supposed to be witty. For some reason, I don't know why, I concluded she was a poetess—another one of Gavin's discoveries. Sometimes, almost in passing, he would put his hand lightly on her arm. As if to draw her closer. As if—perhaps I was only being jealous—to tell me that strangers belonged to him. And because Marion let him do this, I mistrusted her right away.

But I could hardly blame her, because that night—drinking and in favored company—Gavin was in his best form, talking in that remarkable dry voice of his that swooped and soared like an erratic bird: a gift, he used to say, of his Irish ancestors.

"And you see this young fellow here," Gavin said, pointing me out to Marion in his way—charming and condescending. "He can put words in people's mouths and take them out again, like the devil himself." In his more gregarious moments, Gavin liked to lapse into fake dialect. "You see, he's sold a play now for the television, and one day he'll be writing for the stage and screen."

"That's very nice," Marion said.

"Will you listen to her? Who does she think she is?"

"A poetess," I guessed.

Marion laughed, suddenly and abruptly, her open hand slapping the table as she did, her whole docile pose broken apart in this one gesture.

"Guess again," Gavin shouted happily. "You have to guess again."

I appraised her carefully. I could see there was something I had missed: a plain gold ring on her wedding finger.

"A nun," I said. This time only Gavin laughed—and without enthusiasm.

"You're getting worse," he said. "We're going to have to tell you." He leaned over the table and smiled handsomely, the way he had smiled at me in his office, but with that slight added spark which meant he had been drinking for several hours. And even though he looked old and dangerously close to his own thin edge of drunkenness, there was something attractive about his dissipation, about that part of him still an adolescent searching for a wall to crash into. I wondered why he wasn't married—or if, as with his novel, he preferred to make his way slowly through all the possibilities.

"Marion is a producer," he said. "A woman of affairs. She works for a movie company; in fact she owns half of it."

"Gavin tells me you have an idea for a film," Marion said. With her harsh voice she gave the impression of the bank telephoning to announce an overdraft. I looked at Gavin.

"Tell her," he said.

"Well, yes," I mumbled. "Though it's nothing spectacular."

Marion laughed again, so hard that she coughed on her drink. "You have to *pretend* to believe in it," she said. "If you can't, how can I?"

"He's very modest," Gavin offered.

"It's a family habit."

"Tell me about your film."

"Well," I began, "It's about a young man who comes to the city full of dreams—"

"Oh, God," Marion groaned.

"He's only joking," Gavin said. "It's his modesty. Give a writer a few drinks and he's absolutely useless."

"Maybe you should work out the details," Marion said, smiling to tell me she understood what Gavin had done.

"All right," Gavin said. "Next week. Same time, same place. But you have to give us your movie before dinner. No movie, no food." He tipped the bottle and all was forgiven.

* * *

"I have to talk about it," Marion said finally. "You don't mind?"

"I want you to."

"I'll need another drink." This time she waited for me to get it. I brought in the bottle of scotch and the pot of coffee.

"It started a year ago," she said. "He had been having headaches every night and finally I got him to go to the doctor. They did tests, a whole week of tests, and then one day they phoned him up—*over the telephone*—and told him he had a small tumor between his brain and his skull." Her voice shook. She grabbed my arm and then let go. Steady again. *Over the telephone*. So that was how they did it to him. Unfair, because Gavin had more class than that; he always gave the bad news face to face, unafraid of the reaction.

"You remember when we went to Florida last spring?"

"Yes."

"Well, we didn't. We went to Boston and he had the operation. They gave him one chance in five to live—and he made it. Then they told him it might grow there again. They couldn't tell if they had got it all."

"How could he have hidden the operation? They must have had to shave his head?"

"He got a hairpiece. He figured it all out beforehand. Gavin was very clever that way, making things seem proper on the surface." Her hand closed over mine. Not tenderly, or even sadly, but hanging on—squeezing until it hurt. "You know what I mean," she said.

"Sometimes." Her hand over mine. Still wearing the plain gold ring Gavin Donnally had given her fifteen years before, when he'd first asked her to marry him. She had refused him then, but being attached to him and afraid to hurt him, had at least worn the ring. And then, five years later, she took the rest.

"I never loved him," Marion said.

"Of course you did."

"No, I never once loved him, not even for one night."

We were sitting side by side on the couch. After all these years, we were the survivors. We had outlived him; even our betrayals had outlived his honesty. And now Gavin's death was starting to find a place in me, breaking a hole in me as easily as a small mushroom breaks apart a concrete floor.

"I've always told you the truth," Marion said.

"Yes."

Our eyes locked together. There was nothing to shield us from each other now. I remembered how happy Gavin had sounded when he told me they were getting married. His voice then, for once, was neither cynical nor controlled—just happy that finally someone would release him from the contrived pattern of his life. And his eyes, watching mine, already knowing what I was trying to hide.

"He loved you," I said. "He stopped his whole life to let you in."

"I never should have married him."

"Are you sorry?"

Marion's face almost softened. In the months that we were lovers, there were moments when her face looked like this. But now, as then, the look passed quickly. She was learning that with age there is nothing that cannot be hidden. How long was it since she had come here? Minutes, hours—I couldn't tell. I stood up and opened the drapes. Outside, the sky was a deep humid blue.

"I had affairs, you know. And twice I left."

"That's all right." I turned around. She had gotten to her feet and was glaring at me—the old Marion, face impassive and eyes spitting anger.

"I don't need you to forgive me. You of all people." And then suddenly she was across the room, pressed against me.

* * *

The second dinner did not follow the first exactly as planned. Unfortunately, Marion was busy overseeing the funeral of her bankrupt film company. Then, within a month, she had recovered from this disaster and surfaced again as the producer of a series for educational television. Gavin, with his encyclopedic knowledge of matters literary and historical, was made research consultant for the series; and I somehow became responsible for writing the scripts. Soon the three of us were meeting several evenings a week: working, drinking, gossiping and, most of all, listening to Gavin as he talked about anything and everything under the sun.

In those days I was so completely in his spell that I took everything he said as gospel. And Marion, too, seemed utterly hypnotized by him. In his apartment we would sit literally at his feet, taking notes while Gavin reclined in his armchair, retelling the history of the country to us, making it come alive not only as a wild and romantic frontier but also, in some peculiar way, as an enterprise that was *noble* in intent, that took the best of the European experience and matched it up against a continent that could not be touched by even the most extravagant of human excesses. Or so it seemed at the time.

It's hard to look back and say *there* it was. But it is true: it was those few months that made me a writer—the nights spent absorbing another man's way of looking at things, and the mornings and afternoons spent at my typewriter—writing, rewriting, trying to hammer out some sort of script that could mean something to someone else. Of course it was Gavin's vision that I was trying to give, not my own, but I didn't care about that; I only wanted to share the excitement I had started to feel about living in this place, now.

Looking back at myself, I can hardly believe I was ever so unbearably innocent. I thought of myself as an artist, as being utterly sensitive to the smallest nuance of feeling in others. And of course, I was missing everything.

One night, when I was walking Marion home from one of the marathon sessions at Gavin's, she stopped me as we drew in front of her apartment building. "How's the script going?" she asked.

"Fine," I said. This seemed a peculiar question. We had just been talking about it and dissecting it for the last six hours.

"Do you think this is a good way to go about writing, spending so much time talking?"

"What do you mean?" There was about her now a calculating look I hadn't seen since the first night we met. Then I remembered how easily she had survived the failure of her company, and how easily she seemed to manage all the business details of this series, as if, beyond Gavin's living room and romantic stories, there was a world of real fact and solidity where she was absolutely the master.

"I don't know," she said, as if considering all this for the first time. "I mean, this is supposed to be something *you're* doing, you know."

"Don't you think it's good?"

"It's extremely good," she said. "Really."

"You can hire someone else if you want. You shouldn't be stuck with me just as a favor to Gavin."

Marion laughed, in that brusque way of hers, an unsettling sound in the deserted late-night streets. "I'm not like that," she said. "Don't ever think I'm like that."

"I don't," I said. "But if you want to change your mind, now would be a good time to do it."

"Don't worry," Marion said. She looked at me curiously. "Why don't you come up for coffee. I have to go to sleep soon, but you can stay for a few minutes." Her invitation surprised me. Somehow, despite the fact she usually walked home with me, I assumed she belonged to Gavin.

In those days, everything worth having seemed to be Gavin's. His apartment was filled with books, chairs, paintings, ornate rugs —a collector's cave where a man could keep out the world.

Marion's was the opposite. One white wall was faced by a long walnut desk. Her furniture was all hard-edged and expensive, as if planned by an interior decorator on a spaceship theme. In the middle of Marion's desk were ledgers and an adding machine. One almost expected to see production charts and graphs on the wall. Riding up in the elevator, I had thought perhaps she intended to seduce me but, seated in the molded plastic chair with my mug of coffee steaming on the parquet floor, I realized that nothing could be less likely.

"I didn't mean to criticize you," Marion said. "I just thought that we might be taking up too much of your time. Have you been working on anything else, besides the scripts?"

"No."

"Most writers secretly want to do a novel, or a book of short stories."

"I tried that," I said. "Gavin told me that television would suit me better." I felt hurt and betrayed. It was, after all, Gavin who had started these meetings, and Gavin who kept arranging new ones. And if Gavin and Marion wanted to spend time alone, she could have stayed at his place after I left.

"I'm sorry," Marion said. There had always been an easy flow of conversation at Gavin's, but now, alone, we seemed to be at cross purposes. I wanted to leave, and was already thinking about the excuses I would make to Gavin when he telephoned for the next meeting. If we got together once a week it would be enough; then the job would be over and we wouldn't have to see each other again. My coffee wasn't finished but I stood up, glad to be out of her uncomfortable plastic chair.

"I feel tired tonight," Marion said. Her face was impassive as always, but her voice had suddenly changed. Her eyes opened wider. I was standing above her, unsure of what was happening, aware only of the sudden panic that had broken loose in her.

"Please," she whispered. "I'm so tired." She reached out with her hands. I pulled her to her feet, but as soon as she was up she started to lose her balance, and I had to hold onto her to keep her from falling. Half carrying, half dragging her, I got her into the bedroom and onto the bed. It was part of the same fantasy as the rest of the apartment—cold and white. But when I started to leave, Marion held onto me, her fingers digging into my arms. Even as I lay down on the bed I could feel her drifting into sleep, breathing slowly and deeply, her arms tight around me for warmth.

*　*　*

The first signs of dawn were in the room now; a heavy blue light was growing in the center, pushing back the shadows, showing us our faces, pale and exhausted. The bottle stood between us, and we drank from it in little sips and swallows, no longer bothering with ice and water now that we had something we could share: this whiskey, a communion of Gavin's blood thinned to suit our less human veins—Gavin's blood between us, as, for this one moment, we couldn't help believing we had killed him, his death like a curse on all our betrayals, inconsistencies, the tangled web of misunderstandings and desire that had held us together and now kept us apart.

"Do you remember how it was?"

"Yes, I remember Gavin." I felt a growing blackness inside of me, his death, and leaning forward to tip the whiskey into the glass, asked myself, for once, who or what had died for him.

"Not Gavin," Marion said. "You and I. Same scene, same place." She looked at me aggressively, the way Gavin had taught her.

"Of course," I said. Of course, that is, I had done everything possible to forget it. On the morning after that first night, when we woke up fully dressed on her bed, we had looked at each other and without hesitation taken our clothes off and made love: our bodies still warm from each other's arms. And then on nights after that, at my place or hers—always guiltily secret from Gavin—we would spend the late hours together. But it was never as easy and smooth as it had been that first time. The more our bodies needed each other the more our minds and emotions resisted, as if beneath the physical surface we were unable to touch each other. And yet it was still compelling; despite the endless false starts and reservations, there were times we released whole lifetimes of desire.

Then, one day, Marion told me she had also taken Gavin as a lover.

"I see," I said.

"No, you don't."

"I don't want to own you."

"No. But I won't do it again." This admitted half crying, half shouting, enough to bring on more love-making, more of that frantic passion that had first overwhelmed us but now simply pursued us to exhaustion.

We were too much alike, too abrasive. And when we turned in on ourselves, with only our secret to hold us together, we found that it finally wore itself out. Marion arranged to go to England for six months; and I went West. When we came back to Toronto we were both very busy. Our nights together tapered off and the feeling of reunion we should have had never happened. Nor did we ever officially end it. It seemed to just slowly disappear until the time Gavin told me the good news.

"I never forgave you for that last night," Marion said.

"No, I don't suppose you did."

"Maybe we could forget it now, or leave it lie. Gavin was never one for holding grudges."

"No, he wasn't." And now that she had said it, I realized Gavin had never been petty, not Gavin. When he had published his novel—at least Marion had given him the will to overcome that— he dedicated it to both of us, putting us alone, side by side on the same page. As if he knew only he could make a space for us to be together in.

The room was beginning to be light. In another couple of hours, the heat would hang over us again and Gavin's death would start to be incidental to the weather. In the funeral parlor it would be cool enough. They would have his body there by now, and I would have to go to see it.

There is a small porch that leads off my kitchen, suspended twenty feet above the lawn by rotting wooden posts and a few iron braces. We went and leaned precariously over the railing, letting the early-morning air breathe its way around us. Some days I hate the city, it smashes up against me—a concrete jungle of smoke and flesh. And then there are other times, like this, when it lives again for me, and its life presses out of the new air, starting again.

"He killed himself with pills," Marion said. "And then he phoned the ambulance. He didn't want me to come home and find his body—just a note telling me what had happened."

The night before they got married, Marion came over to visit me. One last time, she said, though it had been months since we had spent even an hour alone. Just one last time, but I couldn't. I was feeling too self-righteous and relieved, rehearsing my best man's toast and already involved with someone else. We ended up standing in the middle of my kitchen, half-dressed, shouting at each other. The next day at the wedding, I felt truly close to both of them, assisting with the rings, the champagne, the toasts: finally we had been defined. It was like being released from a long uncertain purgatory.

"I've missed you," Marion said. "Gavin did too. Last week he asked me why we hardly ever saw each other any more. He hated that, old friends slipping away. Secretly he was a crazy optimist. He believed in everyone, even me."

Optimists don't kill themselves, I wanted to say. But didn't. Who knows what people do. Marion's shoulders shook against my arms. She was crying again; and my own tears were starting to gather in the blackness.

"I did love him," Marion said. "I did." Our hands touching, sealed together in the early-morning heat.

A LITERARY HISTORY
OF ANTON

Chapter 1. Anton is born

From the moment that Anton slid out of the bloody canal of his mother and into this world, he was obsessed with the most important question of his life: Who will love me? He cried and shrieked like an infantile prophet. His mother clasped him to her. Even through the fog of anesthetic and pain, she could recognize this voice as part of herself. While she held him, Anton felt his eyelids pressing wetly against his cheeks. For years he woke up this way, crying for no reason. When he was too old to go to his mother, he would lie in bed and wait for the morning to dry his skin.

"At least I was born," he would say. Anton had developed a strange habit of reciting his life to himself, as if he was to be the best proof of his own existence. "At least I was born," he would say. Nothing could release him but the love of a beautiful woman.

Chapter 2. In the afternoon

In the afternoon, Anton liked to meditate upon his mind. He was cultivating that simple and direct clarity which he knew to be the mark of true genius. His eyes learned how to brush themselves in the mirror. Sometimes he dreamed eccentrically; and strolled about the city streets, giving out his innocent and generous smile.

"Anton," his mother said. "You're too old to live at home. It's time you moved out. Your father says you have to be a man."

Anton sighed.

"Well?" his mother asked. "What are you going to do?"

Anton moved to the room above the garage. He kept his curtains closed all the time and began to cultivate newspapers. He fell asleep for a week and no one noticed. When he woke up he inspected himself in the mirror. He spread his hands apart and held them in front of his eyes.

"At least I was born," he said to himself. He dropped out of college and got a job driving a hearse. In the evenings he would go and visit with the inscrutable undertaker.

Chapter 3. Anton meets his destiny (Part One)

Without preamble, after all these years spent sleepwalking through the desert, Anton fell desperately in love. It was everything he had ever imagined: a vise clamping his insides; a symphony of pleasure; an endless trip to the bottom of the bottomless abyss. When he finally landed, there was a journalist waiting to interview him.

MC: Anton, please tell me, everyone wants to know. Is love worth it? Or is it just another game?

A: (groaning). I think my leg is broken. (He feels it carefully, then staggers to his feet.) Where is she?

MC: Anton, I hate to tell you this—but she's gone.

A: Gone? (He clutches his chest and whimpers as he limps about in circles.) I hardly knew her.

MC: Alas, Anton, life is brief. (Takes out note pad and pen.) But you must remember something, all those golden, timeless moments you shared together, the taste of her lips on your tongue, her warm breath on your neck. . . .

A: It began like this. How can I explain? Of those around me, no one but myself believed in love. Pure love. Redeeming love. The utter burning of selfless love. Love. True Love! I spent every day searching for the perfect woman. I didn't care who loved me,

I only wanted to give. One day, when I was in a department store looking for some jewelry to give my poor lonely mother, I absent-mindedly stuffed a few pairs of socks in my coat pocket. (Sometimes, when I am driving at night, my feet begin to sweat.) As I was walking out of the store a premonition of change swept over me. At that very moment my arm was held by a small hand with an iron grip. I turned around. It was love at first sight.

Chapter 4. Intermission

You'll excuse me for interrupting. As you can see, Anton is the type of man who could talk about himself forever. Once started, he finds that his mouth moves with a will of its own, and he babbles compulsively without being able to remember why he began. Of course, self-expression is important. We are pleased to see that Anton is so free with words. But what is there about him that is particularly interesting? Why should we be persuaded that he is a hero of our times?

A hero is a man who is in the vanguard of his own life. He rides it with a kind of foolish resignation, charging bravely into history although it is made up of forces he can neither see nor understand. But Anton waits for his life to happen to him, like a man who has fallen asleep waiting for a bus. Poor Anton, we say, so simple and naïve. What else is there to know?

Chapter 5. Anton meets his destiny (Part Two)

We gazed into each other's eyes. She had grasped my soul, and I hers. We both shuddered at once; fate had crossed our lives, banging them together like two dry bones. During the entire interview with the police our faces were hot scarlet, as if we had been caught performing an obscene act behind the utensils section. Angela was her name.

She had eyes as blue as the sky at dawn. I saw my face reflected and I swam in them, like a fish in the sea.

Heat rose from our skins. Our bodies breathed together, breathed the night in and out. When we heard music, it was music played for us. When our souls joined, they swung together like the sun and the moon.

Chapter 6. The future as history

Looking back, we cannot judge Anton's passion. Although Anton himself is utterly insignificant, it could be that the love that he felt, the passion that briefly transformed him, was somehow universal —and that at least for a brief period Anton was redeemed. So it could be.

So it could be. But as for myself, I don't believe it. To tell the truth, I don't believe in anything about love any more. Sitting here writing about Anton's ridiculous urge to life, I can't help looking out the window. Soon I'll go outside and walk through the streets. The cold concrete will reach up through my shoes, sucking out the warmth of my flesh as the ground beneath turns away from the sun.

What does my life mean? I ask myself. Who cares about Anton? Maybe someone else should be commissioned to write this story. After all, there are at least some interesting moments in his life. There was an incident, for example, that happened while he was working for the undertaker—a brief drama that revealed something about the very inner depths of Anton. It happened one night while they were up late talking.

"Pass the brandy," the undertaker said. He was sitting on his usual casket, the one he used to save money on a couch.

"Of course," Anton replied. He took a long draft from the flask and then passed it to his employer.

"You've worked here one whole year now," the undertaker said. "I want to make you an offer." The undertaker was a tall, sallow man with a deep voice and a masklike face.

"Yes?"

"Suppose I guarantee to you that you will meet the perfect woman of your dreams. You will fall wildly in love with each other. For two weeks everything will be exactly as you have always wished. Even better. Then you will never see her again."

Anton scratched his head. "It sounds attractive—"

"Excellent."

"But I was hoping for something better."

They sat silent for a long time. "You drive a hard bargain," the undertaker finally said. He lit a cigar and puffed at it contemplatively, as if absorbing an unexpected defeat. "You'd better be the one to set the terms."

"A house, to begin with. And more than two weeks. Make it a lifetime, with children and trips to the ocean besides. And, to tell the truth, I've always wanted a sports car and a mistress."

Chapter 7. The whole truth

I want to say first of all that there was no bargain, no deal, no contract or understanding—either under the table or otherwise. I admit that we had a conversation of sorts; it's only natural for people who work together to sometimes pass the day this way. I admit that sometimes the future comes true, but you know that in this and every other interview to the press I've constantly stressed the need—

You know what I mean.

Chapter 8. The interview concluded

MC: Anton?

A: Yes?

MC: I don't think they're coming to rescue us.

A: We're stuck here, then.

MC: When they find us, we'll be dead here at the bottom of the bottomless abyss. Our flesh will have rotted and the birds will have carried our bones away. Only this interview will remain. Do you have any final message? Touching last words?

A: (groaning). There is something I'd like to say—just to you. Promise you won't write it down?

MC: It's getting too dark to see.

A: (hesitantly). Maybe I should have been satisfied with her. I didn't really need a mistress and a sports car. If I would have just stayed at home, everything would have been all right. What do you think?

MC: Me?

A: Yes.

MC: I think you're losing your nerve, Anton. Millions of readers have eagerly followed your adventures, and now you're saying you would have rather stayed home?

A: Yes. That's it exactly.

MC: (after a long silence). Anton, the moon is coming up. Can you see the moon?

A: (groaning). It's beautiful.

MC: I can write by the light of the moon, Anton. Now's the time to say it, to give one last message of hope.

A: I want to thank my parents. . . .

MC: (reading). "In his last, dying moments, the hero of love wished to thank his parents, his wife, and his mistress. He wished them to know that although he died of a broken heart, he suffered no pain, and was looking forward to the great beyond."

BRAIN DUST

It was late, and in the yellow light of a naked bulb Pat Frank wiped his dirty hands on an equally dirty rag, staring abstractedly at his own reflection in the large window of the Salem Garage and General Repair. Briefly he closed his eyes. Blocked gas lines, greasy carburetors, rotted lengths of heater hose swam past in a choked confusion: each coated with layers of soot and dirt, each needing to be replaced but only consigned to him for some temporary and impossible repair, all struggling against the slow ministrations of his big knotted hands. He shook his head and reached below the register for the bottle. Took a drink and remembered something he had seen in the *Reader's Digest,* something about alcohol pickling the brain and making it shrink. He had read this article years before and had since imagined his brain growing smaller and smaller in his big head: first shrinking to the size of a coconut, now a dry rusty orange. Soon it would be like one of those small green tomatoes that lay about in his garden in the fall, planted too late to ripen, skin tough from rain and cold, black frost cracks running along the surface like small dead snakes.

Like snakes, Pat Frank thought, then wondered what his brain, growing smaller, did with the leftovers, if the empty corners in his skull were filled with clouds of brain dust. He wiped the cash register and threw the rag back on the counter. There was something he was supposed to do but he couldn't remember what it was. That was the trouble with taking a new job at his age; after fifty-four years of sleep and drink and shrinkage, the human mind wasn't suited to learning new tasks. Ever since he had started working at the shop, he had been aware of his brain at night; lying in bed, trying to fall asleep quickly so he could wake up before the alarm, he would feel his brain floating restlessly in his skull, the big veins, coming up from the back, trying to find new places to send blood.

Even though the outside signs were off, a truck had driven up and was honking its horn. In the old days, the Salem Garage and General Repair didn't even pump gas; there was more than they could do in fixing farm machinery and installing new furnaces. Now their main business floated through the new pumps that sat conspicuously in the dirt yard, lit day and night by long white neon bulbs.

Pat Frank picked up the rag again and wiped lightly at the counter. The truck door opened, and a man jumped out and started taking his own gas. Through the screen windows Pat could hear the bell ringing off the money; and remembered what he had forgotten—to lock the pump. Friday night. It was Friday night late May, and though the day had been warm the night was cooling fast, clear and threatening to frost.

The nights were his best time now: lying in bed, half asleep and half awake, cool air flowing over him in pulses to match the beating of his heart. It was the way he had lived his nights as a boy, and these nights and those were starting to melt together so that if he was still and breathed slowly, sometimes it seemed that the boy he had been was being born in him again, resurrecting in the body he had given up so long ago but somehow survived anyway—even flourished at times. Like those old trees surrounded by their own dead branches but growing still, new wood circling the old, drinking up the ground in great bursts and exploding into thousands of new leaves every summer. He drank too, Pat Frank did, but from the bottle not the ground; he drank a lot at night but also some during the day, even now, in public, in front of the picture window as the man walked in from the pump to the shop, wallet in hand.

"Pat Frank, you old son of a bitch," he said by way of greeting.

"We were closed," Pat said.

"You was closed, was you? Well, now you're open, you is." The man laughed at his own joke and slapped his money on the counter: a five-dollar bill landing on one of the lazy greasy arborite circles made by the oil rag. "Five dollars even," said the man. "I took five dollars even." He rubbed his face vigorously with the back of his hand, squashing his nose from side to side and snorting up a deep breath. His name was Charlie Malone, and he had a farm—the remains of a farm—a few miles outside of Salem at the end of a dirt road that wound through swamp and bush until it came to Charlie Malone's barnyard, where it died.

Pat Frank put the money in the register and stood opposite Charlie Malone, the black, half-wiped counter between them. Charlie's face was fleshy with snubbed features; and although his blue eyes were round and untouched by time, everything around them was swollen and flushed red. He was a short stubby man. The fair hair he had once had was mostly gone, and even in the spring his scalp was already burned and peeling from the sun. Pat Frank, tall and angular, his bones coming out with age as Charlie's receded into his flesh, could look down at Charlie's skull and see islands of burned skin and new skin. The whole summer, he would look like this: white patches would crop up, be burned, grow white again, as if his whole body's fertility were using his scalp for its final battleground.

"Cold tonight," Charlie offered.

"Cold enough," Pat agreed. And seeing no way to avoid the conversation, he poked his long fingers into the breast pocket of his denim jacket and drew out cigarette tobacco and papers.

"I was thinking of going into town," Charlie said. "You might want to come?"

"Don't know," said Pat. He pulled out the bottle and sat it on the counter. Charlie unscrewed the top, took a big swallow, banged it down against the arborite.

"Son of a bitch," Charlie said. He made a soft choking sound, then coughed hard, clearing his throat. "Jesus Christ, Pat, what is that?" Barclay Three Star Brandy was on the label. Pat grinned at him. Then picked up the bottle and swung it toward his own mouth, his long knobbly arm drawing it gracefully through the air: and for a moment it might have been twenty years ago, when their hair was thick and their muscles were strong and springy, waiting for every Friday night so they could explode into music and dancing and fights, where they mixed their blood and bones with beer and staggered happily out to the morning with the whole world owned and known, sewn into their nerves.

"We could go into town," Charlie said. "I was thinking of it. At least we wouldn't die of the liquor."

"No," Pat agreed. And didn't know how to explain to Charlie Malone—Charlie Malone he had known his whole life and had once found with his leg pinned and broken under a tractor, dying, and gotten him out and to the hospital—that these days he didn't feel like going into town any more. That he didn't exactly feel himself any more, not the way he used to.

"God damn," Charlie said. "It's getting late." He turned his watch out: a big round Timex that told the time in the dark and had the day, too. Five minutes after nine, it said, the hands barely showing through the grease that covered the crystal; grease black and oily like that on Pat Frank's nails and hands—the same, in fact, because only this afternoon they had both had their hands deep in the innards of Charlie Malone's truck, taking out a plugged thermostat, making the engine run cool again. "I don't know if I want to go anyway," Charlie said. "Who do they have tonight?"

"That girl," Pat said. "The one with the green tits." They both laughed and took another turn at the bottle.

Charlie snuffled and rubbed his nose. "Green tits," he said. "I never saw anything like those." He reached for Pat's tobacco and papers and began to roll himself a cigarette. "That reminds me of a story my father used to tell me about your father."

"My father," said Pat, "was above the rabble." Of course there was no story of Charlie Malone's he hadn't heard a hundred times.

"It was about rubber boots," Charlie said. "Did you ever know why your father kept those big rubber boots out in the barn?"

"The barn," Pat repeated, trying to keep up the conversation without listening. Because he was feeling more and more certain that he didn't want to waste this evening with Charlie Malone, standing here at the cash register or in town at the No-Tell Motel, where the girl with green tits sang western music and danced like a cow falling down an icy hill.

"He used to go out and use them for fucking sheep," Charlie said. "He would go out and stand behind them and force their legs into the boots so they would keep still." Charlie smiled at Pat and put the newly made cigarette in his mouth. He had a peculiar and characteristic way of smiling—the Charlie Malone look, people used to call it—a quick movement of the lips that pulled them up at the corners and suddenly exposed his teeth, surprisingly fine and sharp. And Pat Frank was reminded that within the layers of padded flesh and burned-out cells, there still swam the old Charlie Malone, a tough mean boy who liked to fight.

"I never heard that," Pat said. He had a strong bony face, the skin drawn tight by years of incessant drinking, the eyes large and blue, set wide apart and almost frightening to a stranger, burning on either side of his once-broken nose, the whites veined but the pupils absolutely bright and intense, as if they would leap out to swallow everything they saw. As if now, as he leaned toward Charlie Malone and stared at him in the purposeful way, Charlie had smiled, as if trying to see right into Charlie's mind and measure the exact balance of malice and humor, the exact moment they would take this ritual to its next point.

"God damn," Charlie said. He smiled again, his quick fish smile, and spat out the smoke from Pat's tobacco.

At this time of night, still before the tourist season, there were few cars out on the road. Occasionally, one passed the Salem Garage and General Repair. When it did, it slowed momentarily and honked. And each time that happened, Charlie would automatically raise his hand and wave.

"A man needs to keep in practice," Charlie said.

"So they say," said Pat. "If a man's got something to practice with." Charlie Malone and his wife had no children, but Charlie's spinster sister had four. And one by one, as they were born, nurtured and weaned, they were passed over to Charlie's wife in a gesture of many possible meanings.

"Maybe it's getting late," Charlie Malone said. He slapped the counter, a heavy muscled sound as the whole weight of his arm and shoulder flowed through his palm onto the black arborite. In the old days neither of them would have retreated. In the old days they would have driven Charlie's truck to the motel and drunk all night while pretending to listen to the singer with the green tits. Then they would have stepped out to the parking lot: wrestling around in the dirt like schoolboys—looking for vulnerable spots —neck, bellies, ears to be ground into the skull.

"Time to close up," Pat said.

Soon they were outside. The cool air swam around their necks and faces. Pat stuck his long arms straight out like spindles and stretched until his bones cracked into place. He could feel ghosts in the dark air. It was like being asleep. Like being asleep and then waking to feel the night air around him shaped into old friends, so heavy with love his heart felt as if it were being torn apart and poured into the darkness.

"So all right," said Charlie and punched Pat Frank in the shoulder.

"All right," said Pat. "You could drop me at the corners."

To climb into the truck, they had to walk through the clouds of insects attracted by the white glare of the neon gas-pump bulbs. Then the moter started up and they drove away from the Salem Garage and General Repair, Pat pushed way back into the broken upholstery, his feet shoved up under the dash, his hands busy again with papers and tobacco.

After a few miles, Charlie turned off the highway to a dirt road which he drove slowly, trying to save the truck from the worst of its bumps and stretches of washboard. But although in the whole of his fifty-four years Pat Frank had never gotten used to the feeling of being bounced around by the bad roads that surrounded Salem, this one night he was indifferent: because that crazy love that had started to come upon him while he slept and dreamed now poured out of him for Charlie, Charlie Malone, his oldest friend and enemy, Charlie Malone, who was now too old to carry through with his fights, too old to insist they go see a new greentitted singer, too old to do anything but make bad jokes about his father.

When the truck stopped, Pat Frank climbed out, his long legs reaching easily for the ground. "Goodnight," he said. "You sheep-fucking son of a bitch." And while the truck clanked and rattled on its way, throwing up equal amounts of sand and oil, Pat began walking down the long dirt trail that led to Kitty Malone's, sister of Charlie. While he walked he drank the rest of his bottle. The trail—a road really but save for Charlie's truck it was rarely driven—led between long rows of trees, maple and oak, and among the trees were crowded thick clumps of lilac. It was that time of spring when their perfume hangs sweet in the air, overriding everything else, and to Pat Frank that night it was like a wedge driven deep into his chest.

By the time he got within two hundred yards of Kitty Malone's, the dogs had discovered him. While they barked and fussed, Pat walked slowly toward the unlit house, still tasting the last of the whiskey on his tongue. In the sky a half moon was rising. Standing in the middle of Kitty Malone's yard, Pat could see it edged up above the trees, tinged yellow with spring pollen. And as its light seeped around him, running deep grays and blues, he saw Kitty's silhouette growing up out of the shadows of her porch.

"Pat," she said.

"It's me."

He sat down beside her, easing his weight carefully onto the old wood. And took out his tobacco and papers again. Sometimes it seemed whole years were measured out this way: in cigarettes rolled and smoked, in bottles cunningly purchased and consumed, in evenings with Kitty scattered loosely through the seasons. In the light of the moon her skin was a smooth and pale ivory, and there was still a part of him that always gave way to her, that got turned by her presence and utterly captured: as if she were a foreign universe, as if she were still eighteen years old and he thirty-two, already fully expert at hating himself with drink and work, as if it were still the summer of the year she had suddenly become infatuated with him, followed him and Charlie around for three months until finally she found him alone in a field on a night not so different from this. A night when they had suddenly moved from their usual painful conversation to the cold grass, and he was flashing inside her like a long wet snake, the moon lighting up her skin, so smooth then it was like live silk to his tongue.

"Nice night," Pat said. "I got a ride part way with Charlie."

"I heard his truck stop," said Kitty. She leaned close to take the offered cigarette. In the passing of the years her face had changed, but sometimes Pat knew that what seemed to be the bright stony set of her bones was only him seeing his own bitterness written on her face.

They sat quietly on the porch.

He reached out and took her bare foot in his hand, pressed his palm into her arch until he heard her sigh with pleasure. Then her other foot, his hands kneading it until it, too, relaxed to his touch.

"Pat," she said. "I don't feel so good tonight."

"What's wrong?"

"I don't know."

He rested her feet in his lap and tapped the ash off his cigarette. Her words, the tone of her voice, found a familiar place in him— the kind of feeling he had learned to recognize long before and knew how to surround with brandy and wine.

"I'm sorry," she said. "I knew you would be coming tonight." Since he had started working at the garage he had spent most of his weekends with her—as if after all these years of unemployment his unexpected job earned him other rights too.

He stood up slowly on the porch and stretched his arms straight out. His bones couldn't respond. The moon was higher in the sky now, had turned from yellow to pure ice-white. Everything was shrinking, he thought: the moon, his brain, his times with Kitty Malone. The only thing that was growing was his heart, and it just seemed to be getting crazy and sentimental.

"You don't have to go," said Kitty. "I'd like you to stay."

"Anyone else here?"

"Only Lynn. She went to sleep early." She stretched out a foot to touch Pat's trousers. "She made me promise you'd be here in the morning."

"Okay," Pat said. "What's wrong?"

"I don't know."

In the old days her moods had destroyed him: he would feel completely caught up in her, given over, and then suddenly she would be gone. His first reaction was to drink away his anger. And then he got so furious he refused to drink, but spent whole nights walking about, the frustration roiling through his guts and blood.

"You want some tea?" Kitty said. "I don't have anything else except that wine."

"Tea." The fall past, in a week of reconciliation, they had made grape wine together. The week ended, they had a fight, its shadow fell over the wine, which turned into sour red vinegar unacceptable by even the most desperate of standards.

They went into the kitchen and switched on the light. They looked almost like brother and sister, these two, both tall and strong-boned, molded in the image of the harsh seasons and infertile land. But where Pat had devoured his flesh by drinking and turned his cheeks into caverns, Kitty still kept signs of youth. She would be forty in the fall and had borne four children, but her body seemed to have survived well enough. The years had added a forward slope to her shoulders and small layers of flesh and fat, but her face was honed and optimistic; and Pat could see she was still looking forward even as he was sliding back.

On top of one of the counters was a Coleman stove. Kitty pumped it up and set a kettle on top. They were so used to their fights they didn't have to follow them through any more. Like a mud-bedded river, they flowed around the sore spots and let the channels cut deep where the going was soft.

Sitting at the kitchen table, they might have been any married couple: but they weren't. In the two decades of their time, their nights together might have filled out two years.

"You have a good week?" Kitty asked.

"Not bad." His hands kept wanting to shake but he knew how to control them. He wished he had saved the whiskey instead of sharing it with Charlie Malone. He wanted to be at his own house, sitting on his own front step with the bottle in his hand, the sound of his brother's sleeping in the air, and the moon shining down on him alone.

He looked unhappily at Kitty and shook his head. His plan had been that he would come to see her tonight and they would lie in her bed and make love until he was so drunk and tired he could feel like he was floating, and then he was going to tell her about his brain getting smaller and leaving bits of dust in the corners of his skull. That was what he had wanted. To tell her about his brain and the boy he was growing into. If that had happened, he thought, sipping forlornly at his tea, if that had happened he could have forgiven the rest, everything they had missed.

"You want to know what I did this week? I went to see the doctor."

"You did," said Pat.

"I was three months late."

Pat found himself counting back in his head, to remember if he had been with her then; and located the memory of a week they had spent together in the last of the winter, when he had felt so depressed and unhappy he could do nothing with himself except walk the twelve miles through the wet snow from his own place to hers—and present himself at her door to be cured. As always, she had taken him in, made him feel so loved he had forgotten how it was he had ever felt anything else. And remembering this gift, as he sat at her table now, watching her pour tea in anticipation of this new pregnancy, his heart opened up the way it had earlier in the evening with Charlie Malone, an emotional spasm he couldn't control. But this time instead of love alone it was laced with a complete revulsion at the sight of himself sitting at the table of this woman and counting back the months as if he owned her.

"He said I wouldn't be having any other babies. Nothing to worry about. He said there's a big cyst on one of my ovaries and when they take it out they'll take everything else, too. So I don't have to worry."

Her cigarette had gone out. She lit it again and sipped at a new cup of tea. Her eyes held to his. Then she exhaled, long and slow, as if she had been holding her breath.

"I'm sorry."

"It's all right."

Their hands reached for each other and met in the middle of the table. His was large and bony, swollen-knuckled, still marked by grease from the garage. Hers was short-fingered and wide, the skin rough, the nails bitten and jagged.

Without speaking, they got up, turned out the light, and walked through the dark house to her bedroom. There they lay down on their backs, still holding hands.

"Sometimes I wonder," said Kitty, "if we did the right thing."

The gap in his heart opened wider. It was trying to cry from the inside. He had something important to say, but he didn't know what it was: he could only feel in his brain the sogged and paralyzed cells that were trying to rise to the occasion. He and Kitty had spent five years meeting secretly and not-so-secretly, in fields and barns. He believing all the time that he was too old for her, that she must leave him. But when she had finally moved to the city, married, had her first two children, he learned to hate himself for refusing to reach for her. And when she came back she didn't want to be reached—not that way; she had landed in the middle of her own life.

They fell asleep holding hands. And woke up in each other's arms, taking off each other's clothes. Her back arched under his wide hand, his tongue found the soft spot in the center of her throat. But as he was about to go in her she stiffened and went tight.

"What's wrong?"

"I don't know."

"Did the doctor hurt you?"

"No." She drew away. "Sometimes I don't know what you want."

"I wanted you," Pat Frank said. "I wanted all of you." He was sure that if he had the brandy now he would be drinking it and keeping quiet. He sat up in the bed and reached for tobacco and papers. "Forget I said that."

"It's all right," Kitty said. "I wanted you, too." She sat up beside him. With the years and the children, her once-taut stomach had grown into a double balloon. "Don't upset yourself," she said. "It's best to take things as they are."

"We'll be dead soon enough," Pat said sarcastically, and that familiar sour feeling was jumping through him.

"Don't say that."

"I'm sorry." And in fact he didn't believe that either of them was close to dying. She would survive the operation as easily as she survived everything else. And as for himself, the worst thing was that on these nights when he melted into the boy he used to be, the boy who had been full of dreams and hopes, on these nights he felt as if he would live forever.

* * *

The light was beginning to come up. Pat put on his clothes, went outside, and started the long walk home. It was still before sunrise and the grass was blue-green, wet and shining like the sea. He hadn't looked back at her, he hadn't looked back. He was fifty-four years old. As he walked through the wet grass his boots turned black and soaked through.

The first time they had been together, when the first sex was over and the evening still lived in them, he had gotten up on his knees and licked her from the cleft between her legs to her throat, in a long straight line that his tongue could still feel, live silk, a long straight line from that moment to now, and then from her throat to her lips, which he could still taste, sweet and warm to his tongue, drinking it in till the roots ached.

He walked slowly, unsure of what he was walking away from, and while he walked he was aware of the dogs coming with him, barking occasionally to advertise to the others a treed porcupine or a groundhog hole, out of sight most of the time but now and then crossing his path for a touch or a word.

He went off the trail and up through the maple trees and the lilac, where he often liked to sit and watch the sun come up. Now it was still hovering below the horizon; but it was sending light up into the sky in long white-yellow fingers that expanded into giant shafts of brightness, turning the whole sky into a giant domed cathedral, into the cover of a crazy religious magazine.

And while this light shot up in the sky as if God's voice were going to suddenly open up and make His final speech, the barking of the dogs grew louder and more insistent, the tones of excitement and discovery giving way to shrill yelps of pain and fear, until Pat stood up, returned his half-rolled cigarette to the package and began to lope toward the noise, already hearing in it the cries of whatever the dogs had caught. He had to go down to the trail and across it, up another small hill and through a tangle of young maple and oak—and then he was there: in a clearing where the dogs, five of them, were fighting with a giant raccoon.

They were all of them covered in each other's blood, and the raccoon's screaming had grown into a human voice. Four of the dogs, their mouths and noses cut by the claws, had hold of the raccoon's legs and were stretching it out in the air; the fifth—an old hound that lay around the yard all day—was rushing back and forth, her head jerking forward convulsively, like a bird's head, stabbing down into the raccoon's belly and ripping it out in long sharp bites.

"Stop it," Pat Frank yelled. "Fuck off, you god-damned dogs." And was bending down to find rocks to throw. But the dogs paid him no attention—they were immune to his voice, to stones bouncing off their faces, even to his kicks as he came close and tried to pull them away. They barked to each other and they hung onto the raccoon, crazily excited, dancing around in their morning circle, dancing and pulling out the raccoon as they danced, holding it high in the air as its blood squirted out all over them and its screams cut open the morning.

Pat turned around and ran. Through the trees and down the hill to the trail. And along the trail, feeling his feet squish in his soaking socks and boots, his lungs raw and straining for more air, ran until he got to the edge of the yard, where he stopped to get his breath. The cool morning air struggled with the sweat on his skin. The rising sun turned the grass and leaves a lemon green. Pat Frank wiped the blood from his hands, finished rolling his cigarette, and walked toward the house of Kitty Malone. She was sitting on the porch, as if she had been waiting for him, sitting in the same place she had been a few hours before, and as he came close to her the smell of dew and lilacs was mixed with coffee.

He handed her the cigarette and sat down opposite her.

"It's next week," Kitty said.

"I'll drive you down."

"You don't have to. Charlie could."

He lit her cigarette, then rolled one for himself. He wanted to ask her something about the baby she might have had. He couldn't hear the dogs any more. "Maybe I'll have some of that wine," Pat Frank said. "It can't be that bad."